COOPER'S CORNER CHRONICLE

Wanted: Cooper's Corner's Most Romantic Couple

Valentine's Day is just around the corner and it's time once again for the annual Sweetheart Dance. Members of the dance committee have been working hard to make this year's event a fun-filled evening for young and old, singles and couples. According to organizer Phyllis Cooper, there'll be a live band, and Cupid will be on hand to work his magic.

Raffle tickets are being sold the week before the dance, and the winner will be treated to a haircut and makeup by the talented—and generous—Rowena Dahl of A Cut Above. The highlight of the dance will be the selection of Cooper's Corner's most romantic couple. Of course, our little town has lots of candidates, given the run on weddings we've had lately. But a warning to the younger generation: you'll have stiff competition from those longtime romantics Phyllis and Philo Cooper, Lori and Burt Tubb, and Martha and Felix Dorn.

No date is required, so don't pine away at home when you could be having the time of your life at the Sweetheart Dance. And who knows? Your very special Valentine could be waiting for you there!

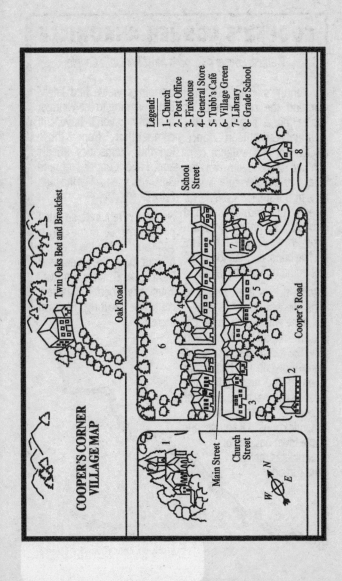

COOPER'S CORNER

KRISTIN GABRIEL

Accidental Family

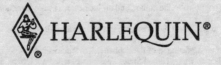 HARLEQUIN®

TORONTO • NEW YORK • LONDON
AMSTERDAM • PARIS • SYDNEY • HAMBURG
STOCKHOLM • ATHENS • TOKYO • MILAN • MADRID
PRAGUE • WARSAW • BUDAPEST • AUCKLAND

For Carolyn Greene,
great author and dear friend

HARLEQUIN BOOKS
225 Duncan Mill Road, Don Mills,
Ontario, Canada M3B 3K9

ISBN 0-373-61257-5

ACCIDENTAL FAMILY

Kristin Gabriel is acknowledged as the author of this work.

Visit us at www.eHarlequin.com

Printed in U.S.A.

Dear Reader,

I live in a village about the size of Cooper's Corner, so I'm familiar with both the joys and the trials of small-town life! The sense of community is wonderful, and I hope the people of Cooper's Corner become as real for you as they have for me.

When a big-city boy meets a small-town girl in *Accidental Family*, it doesn't take long for the whole town to discover their secret.

I hope you enjoy Alan and Rowena's story!

All my best,

Kristin Gabriel

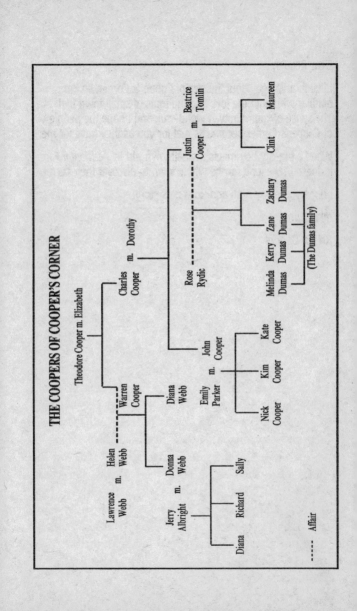

THE COOPERS OF COOPER'S CORNER

Theodore Cooper m. Elizabeth

Warren Cooper ----- Helen Webb (m. Lawrence Webb)

Charles Cooper m. Dorothy

Justin Cooper m. Beatrice Tomlin

Diana Webb

Donna Webb (m. Jerry Albright)

Diana — Richard — Sally

Emily Parker m. John Cooper

Nick Cooper — Kim Cooper — Kate Cooper

Rose Rydic ----- Justin Cooper

Melinda Dumas — Kerry Dumas — Zane Dumas — Zachary Dumas

(The Dumas family)

Clint — Maureen

----- Affair

CHAPTER ONE

IT WAS the longest five minutes of her life.

Rowena Dahl paced back and forth in the small examination room, waiting for the nurse to return with the results of the test. Ironically enough, she'd been placed in one of the rooms usually reserved for children. A mural of hot air balloons adorned one bright yellow wall. An oversize teddy bear sat in a toy high chair in one corner of the room, a bandage covering the top of his button nose, and a Mr. Potato Head perched on top of the file cabinet.

A baby's sudden cry carried through the thin walls, then quieted to a whimper. The waiting room was packed today, and nurses were rushing up and down the long hallway. At first the nurse had mistakenly thought she'd come in for a flu shot, until Rowena nervously explained the real reason for her visit.

She smiled to herself as she bent to pick up the teddy bear, then squeezed it tight against her chest. She'd been filled with second thoughts when she'd made that fateful trip to Toronto last October, worried she might be making a big mistake. But now, almost three months later, she knew in her heart that the only mistake was waiting so long to try and make her dream come true.

"Please," Rowena prayed under her breath. "Please let me be pregnant."

Her cycle had become more and more irregular over the last couple of years and set off the alarm on her biological clock. Especially when the doctor had warned this might be a sign of early menopause.

At thirty-six, she'd sifted through too many Mr. Wrongs to believe she'd ever find a Mr. Right. Maybe she was too picky. Or simply too stubborn to give up her independence. Either way, she couldn't afford to wait for her true love to find her any longer. She had to take matters into her own hands.

With the help of her doctor, she'd chosen a reputable fertility clinic in New York City. When that didn't take, her doctor recommended a specialty clinic in Toronto that offered a new, highly successful procedure. That's where she found her perfect match. The sperm donor was forty years old, a physicist who had played semipro baseball just out of college. His medical history was clean, no genetic defects or serious diseases. According to the sperm donor profile, his hair was blond, like her own, and his eyes blue. Although he was identified only by a number, she knew the man was six feet tall, average weight and of French Canadian descent. She'd taken great care in selecting the father of her baby.

She just hoped he was fertile.

The Orr Fertility Clinic performed the insemination procedure in October. When Rowena began spotting in November, she believed it had failed. But when she'd missed her period altogether in December, she began to wonder if the procedure had been a success after all.

Suspecting she might be pregnant, she could barely restrain herself from running down to Cooper's Corner General Store to buy a home pregnancy test. But with either Philo or Phyllis Cooper manning the cash register, there would have been no way to keep such a purchase secret. So she'd decided to wait until she could make an appointment with Dr. Milburn in Williamstown. A wait that had stretched into the first week of January and now seemed interminable.

The door opened, and her heart leaped in her chest. But instead of the nurse, Dr. Milburn himself stepped inside. A general practitioner in his late fifties, he specialized in pregnancies and deliveries. She liked the faint, comforting aroma of pipe tobacco surrounding him that reminded Rowena of her grandfather. Dr. Milburn had always been so kind, competent and supportive that she'd chosen to stay with him rather than seek the services of an obstetrician.

He pulled a pair of bifocals out of the front pocket of his white lab coat. "Good afternoon, Rowena. Sorry to keep you waiting."

"Looks like you're busy today." Realizing she was still holding the teddy bear, she hastily placed it on the high chair. Then she turned to face him, surprised to find her knees shaking.

"I'm never too busy to see one of my favorite patients." He opened her file. "Go ahead and have a seat."

She lowered herself into her chair, her gaze never leaving his face. Dr. Milburn didn't say anything for several long seconds, and the expression on his face made her uneasy. He'd told her that for a woman her age, the chances of conceiving through artificial insemination were between sixty and seventy percent. That was one of the reasons Rowena had waited so long before she'd made the appointment. She'd been afraid of getting her hopes up prematurely, even with encouraging signs lately, like early morning nausea and occasional dizziness.

But what if she wasn't pregnant? What if these symptoms were all in her imagination? Rowena couldn't stand the suspense any longer. "Do you have the results of my pregnancy test?"

"Yes," he murmured, still studying her chart. Then he cleared his throat and looked at her. "Congratulations, young lady. You're going to be a mother."

She blinked, almost afraid to believe it. "Really? But how is that possible? I was spotting in November."

"That's not too unusual in early pregnancy." A gentle smile creased his face. "There's no doubt about it, Rowena. The test came back positive. Since you had the procedure done in mid-October, that makes you about twelve weeks along already."

A surge of joy shot through her, and her eyes blurred with tears. "I can't believe it. This is so…" But she couldn't put her feelings into words. After so many years of living on her own, she was finally going to have a family again. To the outside world, her life probably seemed perfect. She owned a successful business and a comfortable home in the small village of Cooper's Corner, Massachusetts. But she'd been so alone for so long.

"Here," Dr. Milburn said, reaching over to hand her a tissue.

"I've never been happier," she said at last, wiping her wet cheeks with the tissue. "Thank you."

He sighed. "I hope you'll still feel that way when you hear what I have to tell you."

Apprehension fluttered through her. "What?"

"I was hoping we wouldn't need to have this discussion," he began, then took off his bifocals and folded them in his hand. "But I'm afraid it's unavoidable now."

Her fingers gripped the armrests as she prepared herself for another roller-coaster ride. "Please just tell me, Dr. Milburn. Is something wrong?"

"There was a problem with the insemination procedure. A mistake, actually."

"A mistake?" she echoed.

"Nothing to be too alarmed about," he assured her. "My office discovered it when the clinic sent a copy of your records here."

"I still don't understand."

He hesitated for a long moment. "It turns out that you were not inseminated with the donor sperm you selected, Rowena."

She stared at him, trying to make sense of his words. "How can that be possible?"

"I wish I knew." He closed her file. "In my experience with the Orr Fertility Clinic, they have stringent verification procedures. That's one of the reasons I recommended them to you. Unfortunately, a fluke occurred in your case, due either to human error or some kind of computer malfunction. I've contacted the clinic and they're naturally very concerned and trying to discover the source of the mix-up.''

She didn't care about the Orr Clinic. She cared about her baby. "So who is the donor?"

He lifted his narrow shoulders. "That's something that may remain a mystery. Apparently, there is no profile available on the man. At least, not one that has been discovered yet.''

She looked at him in disbelief. "You don't know *anything* about him?"

"I'm afraid not.''

She took a deep breath and tried to comprehend what he'd just told her. She'd spent countless hours picking out the perfect father for her baby, and now fate had stepped in and taken that choice away from her.

Concerned by her silence, Dr. Milburn leaned forward and placed his hand over hers. "I know this is quite a shock, but let me assure you that all the donations to the Orr Clinic are required to undergo rigorous screening for medical and genetic defects, as well as all sexually transmitted diseases. The specimens are quarantined for a minimum of six months to ensure the safety of the patients receiving them. There's absolutely no reason to believe you won't deliver a perfectly healthy baby.''

She barely heard him. "So it could be anyone.''

"Yes," he confirmed. "It could be anyone.''

A strange numbness enveloped her. But despite her shock, she still wanted this baby—more than anything.

He stood up. "Give yourself some time, Rowena. I'm going to skip my usual first pregnancy spiel because I think you have enough to handle right now. But I'd like to see you again in two to three weeks, and we'll go from there. In the meantime, I'm going to prescribe some prenatal vitamins for you."

She nodded, her mind still grappling with the news he'd just given her. Choosing to become a single mother hadn't been an easy decision. She'd weighed all the pros and cons. Considered all the possible scenarios.

Except this one.

She'd even taken some comfort in the thought that she could picture the donor in her mind. His blond hair. His blue eyes. His six-foot frame standing in the batter's box. Maybe it was silly, but it had made the whole procedure seem a little less impersonal.

Now the image she had of her baby's father was a blank. An awful, fuzzy blank. She didn't know anything about him—his height, his background, his occupation. Not even an identification number.

The doctor stood and walked to the counter, then scribbled out a prescription on his pad. He tore off the top sheet and handed it to her. "Here you go. You can schedule your next appointment with the receptionist on your way out."

"All right," she replied automatically.

He started to say something, then turned and walked out the door without another word.

Rowena placed her hand over her abdomen. Before long she'd begin showing. The baby inside her would be oblivious to a world of sperm donors and medical mix-ups and French Canadian baseball players. This baby needed her.

Almost as much as she needed it.

ALAN RAND'S HEART raced as he eased himself into the shallow end of the indoor swimming pool. Taking a deep breath of chlorine-scented air, he forced himself to let go of the concrete edge. He knew it was ridiculous for a thirty-four-year-old man to be terrified of the water, but waves of panic lapped at him like the tepid water against his bare chest.

Light from the January sun shone through the opaque windows and reflected off the surface of the pool, making him wince at the brightness. The young instructor, a woman just out of her teens, dove into the pool on the opposite end and gracefully swam to where her small class of beginning adult swimmers stood gathered together in the water.

She pushed the wet hair out of her eyes, then flashed a toothy smile at her wary students. "Good afternoon. Is everybody ready for our second lesson?"

Alan forced himself to nod along with the rest of the class.

"Okay," she said, effortlessly treading water as if she preferred swimming to standing. "Let's get started with ten bobs."

Alan swallowed the fear that threatened to choke him, then took a deep breath and plunged into the water. A moment later, he broke the surface for another gasp of air. He swiftly bobbed up and down nine more times, not allowing his irrational phobia to overwhelm him. He'd faced much worse.

If he could beat cancer, he could do anything.

That was one of the reasons he was here today. After his diagnosis three years ago, he'd made a list of everything he'd wished he'd done in his life. Things like mountain climbing, and flying to Venice, and learning to swim. Ever since his recovery, he'd been methodically going through that list, determined to accomplish everything on it.

He bobbed into the water an eleventh time, then a twelfth, pushing himself past the limit. It was how he intended to live his life from now on. Both at his work as a senior editor for a successful Toronto publishing company as well as in his personal life. No more standing on the sidelines for Alan Rand.

When he bounced out of the water for the fifteenth time, he saw a familiar face smiling at him. Bradford Haley, Jr., his old friend and lawyer, stood in a suit and tie on the wet tile floor next to the edge of the pool.

"I called your office, and your secretary told me I could find you here," Brad said.

Alan heaved himself out of the swimming pool, relief flooding him at the unexpected reprieve. He grabbed a fluffy white towel with the words Flemingdon Aquatic Centre emblazoned across it in blue letters. He swiped the towel over his face as water ran off his body and down his long legs. His black swimming trunks clung to his hips in a way that left little to the imagination. The instructor stood staring at him until he caught her gaze. Then she hastily looked away, a blush on her freckled cheeks.

Brad smiled. "Still impressing the ladies, I see."

"They really love it when I flail around in the pool and pretend I'm drowning," he said wryly. "So what brings you here, Brad?"

"You told me to contact you as soon as I had any information on your case."

"And you probably wanted an excuse to skip out on a boring meeting."

Brad grinned. "You know me too well."

"So what did you find out?" Alan asked.

"I'm afraid the news isn't good. I contacted the Orr Fertility Clinic as you requested, but they were apparently unable to locate your, uh…"

"Deposit," Alan supplied the word, knowing Brad was curious about why his friend would go to a sperm bank in the first place.

"Right," Brad said. "Anyway, when I finally convinced them they could either tell me now or wait until they received a subpoena, they relented. Of course, they can't release any medical records because of confidentiality laws, but I was able to see their financial records."

Alan tensed. "And?"

"And on October eighteenth of last year, a woman from Massachusetts purchased deposit number two eight four six."

Dread filled him. "My number."

Brad nodded. "If it makes any difference, the Orr Clinic apologized profusely for the mistake and told me the employee responsible will be fired."

"I don't want their apologies," Alan said, his voice rising. "I just want to know what the hell some strange woman is doing with my sperm!"

His words echoed over the pool, and his classmates all stopped swimming to gape at him.

"I think that's obvious," Brad said softly, as they both turned away from the pool.

A chill swept over Alan's wet body. "She wants a baby."

Brad cleared his throat. "I take it you didn't intend for your deposit to be donated?"

"No." Alan hadn't told anyone about his visit to the Orr Fertility Clinic. Three years ago, most of his friends had been worried about climbing the corporate ladder or buying the latest sports car. Few of them knew about his battle with Hodgkin's disease, but those that did, like Brad, couldn't help but reveal their uneasiness around him. Hell, he'd been uneasy, too. And scared as hell.

When the oncologist had advised him to make a deposit at a sperm bank in case the treatments left him sterile, he'd done it without question. Then he'd forgotten all about it until the day he'd received a telephone call from the Orr Fertility Clinic in early January. That's when this nightmare had begun.

"Tell me what you know about this woman," Alan said as the class behind him began to practice back-floats.

Brad shrugged. "Not much. Her name is Rowena Dahl. She lives in a small town in Massachusetts. In October, she came to Toronto and paid a visit to the Orr Clinic, which means she probably had the insemination procedure done here."

"Is she married?" Alan wondered if a husband's infertility had brought her to the clinic.

"No," Brad replied. "Single."

Alan hesitated, his next question sticking in his throat. "Is she pregnant?"

Brad shrugged. "The clinic didn't have that information, or won't release it. They're worried about the legal ramifications, of course."

As a businessman, Alan understood their concern. As a man, he just wanted to punch somebody. He wasn't ready to become a father. Certainly not with a woman he'd never met before. Having a child was definitely on his list, but so far down he hadn't even thought about it. Until now.

"Look," Brad said, "this really isn't your responsibility. Especially since you never intended for your deposit to be donated. If this woman is pregnant, then she went into the situation with her eyes wide open. You can turn around and walk away with a clear conscience."

Alan wished it were that easy. But he simply wasn't made that way. Not when he knew firsthand how it felt to grow up with a father who didn't care. George Rand had lived in the same house but had never participated in his son's life. He could never be bothered to attend Alan's soccer games or the school play or take him to movies. When they were in the same room together, his father would often hide behind a newspaper, answering Alan's questions with little more than monosyllabic grunts.

By the time he was a teenager, Alan and his father barely spoke to each other. Two strangers living in the same house, with his mother as their intermediary. She died five years ago, and her funeral was the last time he'd set eyes on his father. George Rand had moved to Albany, New York, shortly afterward, and Alan didn't even have his telephone number.

Alan might never have known how a real father acted if he hadn't spent so much of his childhood with Brad's family. He'd watched Mr. Haley cheer on his children in whatever they did. In success or failure. He offered advice, discipline and hugs in equal measure. A father like Mr. Haley would have stayed by his son's side during radiation treatments. He would have at least made a damn phone call.

"What's the name of the town this woman lives in?" Alan asked.

"Cooper's Corner." Brad tilted his head. "I take it you're not going to walk away?"

"I need to know if she's pregnant with my baby."

"Why don't you let my office handle it," Brad suggested. "Save yourself the trip."

Alan shook his head. This was too important to leave to his lawyers. He wanted to see her for himself. Size her up before he made his next move. "This is my problem. It will take me a couple of weeks to clear off my desk at the office, then I'll be on my way."

"Look on the bright side," Brad said with a wry smile. "You'll get a break from these swimming lessons you love so much."

Alan nodded, but at the moment the Olympic-size swimming pool seemed much safer than the dangerous waters waiting for him. Just the thought that Rowena Dahl might be carrying his baby made him feel as if he'd been dumped in the middle of Lake Ontario.

It was up to him to sink or swim.

CHAPTER TWO

ROWENA MANAGED to keep the news of her pregnancy a secret for almost three weeks before she finally needed to confide in someone. Knowing she could trust her friend Maureen Cooper, she found herself sitting in the warm, cozy kitchen of the Twin Oaks Bed and Breakfast on a wintry Sunday evening in late January.

"So now you've heard the whole story," Rowena said. "I'm pregnant and I know absolutely nothing about the father of my baby."

"I can't believe a reputable clinic would make that kind of mistake." Maureen, who owned Twin Oaks with her brother, Clint, handed Rowena a mug of hot tea then sat down at the table. Three years younger than Rowena, Maureen stood close to six feet tall and wore her long chestnut hair pulled back in a simple ponytail.

"It's taken me a while to believe it myself." Rowena wrapped her hands around the warm mug. "In fact, I've been having nightmares about it."

"You look as if you haven't been sleeping well," Maureen admitted. "Have you been eating?"

Rowena shrugged. "To tell you the truth, I haven't had much of an appetite."

Without another word, Maureen got up and walked to the pantry. A moment later she was back at the table with two plates, each holding a huge frosted roll. "No one can resist my brother's homemade cinnamon rolls."

Clint Cooper was an accomplished chef and locally famous in the Berkshires for his fabulous breakfast buffets at Twin Oaks.

"I can't eat all this," Rowena protested as Maureen set a plate and fork in front of her.

"Just eat as much as you can," Maureen replied, sitting across the table from her. "The baby needs it as much as you do."

A twinge of guilt jabbed Rowena as she picked up the fork. She had to eat properly, even if food did taste like sawdust in her mouth. But rather than resurrect the nausea that had haunted her for the last few weeks, the first bite of cinnamon roll melted on her tongue. "This is absolutely delicious."

Maureen smiled, then dug into her own roll. "I thought you'd like it. I remember when I was pregnant with the twins, I ate just about everything in sight. I gained almost fifty pounds."

Rowena smiled, finding it hard to picture the svelte Maureen heavy with pregnancy. A little of her anxiety lessened as she thought of Randi and Robin Cooper. The adorable three-year-olds were well-behaved and so sweet. She needed to concentrate on the baby she'd be bringing into this world and stop worrying about the man who had fathered it.

Easier said than done.

She wouldn't be able to hide her pregnancy much

longer. Right now bulky sweaters covered her expanding stomach. But soon there would be maternity clothes to buy and questions to answer as her condition became obvious. Questions she still wasn't sure how to answer.

"Any morning sickness?" Maureen asked.

"Just a little queasiness." She swirled her fork in the icing on her cinnamon roll. "Although I did almost faint in church this morning. Dr. Dorn was there and took me out into the narthex. He was quite concerned until I told him about my condition."

Maureen smiled at the mention of the retired elderly doctor. "Did he ask you about the father?"

"No, although I'm sure he was curious." She sighed, then muttered, "Aren't we all?"

Maureen took a sip of her tea. "You don't know *anything* about him?"

Rowena shook her head, the fears that had been keeping her awake at night rising once again to the surface. "Absolutely nothing. The clinic is refusing to reveal any information because of the possibility of a lawsuit."

"Don't they realize how unfair this is to you?" Maureen asked, indignation blazing in her green eyes. "I think you should file a lawsuit."

"I thought about it," Rowena admitted, "but the last thing I want is for this story to hit the newspapers. Especially if my name is revealed." She shook her head. "I never want my child to someday discover he or she was conceived as the result of a mistake."

Maureen nodded. "I understand. But I still think

the Orr Clinic could be a little more cooperative. At least give you some kind of description of the man.''

''They claim this particular donor never filled out a profile. Which means the father of my baby could be an eighteen-year-old college student or a sixty-year-old grandfather. Any age. Any nationality. He could be a drug addict or a felon. He could be mentally unstable or have some serious genetic defect.''

Maureen held up her hand. ''Whoa, slow down. You don't have any reason to think the worst. I've heard that most sperm donors are medical students. Surely the clinic had a rigid screening program.''

''So Dr. Milburn said, but how can I be certain?'' She took a deep breath, knowing from personal experience that even seemingly normal men could have serious problems. That was one of the reasons she'd moved to Cooper's Corner six years ago. ''I've already talked to my attorney, and he's promised to push the clinic for more information.''

''Well, that's good.''

''The point is, the father of my baby could be *anyone*. I'm still single because I've been waiting for Mr. Right to come along before I started a family. Now, instead of Mr. Right, I'm stuck with Mr. Anonymous.''

''But you didn't know the other sperm donor, either,'' Maureen gently reminded her. ''Other than what you learned from his profile.''

She sighed. ''I know. I must sound ridiculous. It's just that I've wanted a baby for so long, and now that I'm pregnant it seems as if there are so many things to worry about.''

Maureen laughed. "Welcome to motherhood."

Rowena gave her a wry smile. "Why didn't anyone tell me it was going to be this much fun?"

"It will be," Maureen promised, a soft glow in her green eyes. "The only thing you need to concentrate on for the next few months is bringing a healthy baby into the world. And the first time you hold your new baby in your arms, you'll know it's worth all the worry in the world."

Tears stung Rowena's eyes. She couldn't let her worry overcome the miracle of the child inside her. "I have to admit I'm a little nervous. I've got textbooks on pregnancy and childbirth piled three feet high on my nightstand. The one I'm reading now says I should feel the baby start to move soon. But there's so much I don't know. So much I need to learn."

"Most of it just comes naturally," Maureen assured her. "The rest you'll learn along the way. And you know that I'll be here to help."

"Thanks." Rowena's throat grew tight. Hormones had made her emotions more unsteady than usual, and tonight they were right on the surface. "That means a lot to me."

"Does anyone else know about your pregnancy?"

She shook her head, then emitted a tight laugh. "I obviously won't be able to keep it a secret forever."

"Well, I won't tell anyone," Maureen promised. "This is your news."

"It's more like a tabloid story," Rowena quipped, scraping the last bits of icing off her plate. "But you can tell Clint if you want. And make sure you tell him

I have an insatiable craving for cinnamon rolls, too.''

Maureen laughed. "You got it."

LATER THAT EVENING, Maureen stood at the front window, watching Rowena drive off into the snowy darkness. She wished there was some way she could assure her that everything would be all right. But there were no guarantees in life. She couldn't imagine not knowing the identity of the father of her twin girls. Randi and Robin had their father's blue-green eyes and easy smile. She and Chance had been so in love once, until he'd moved to Paris.

If only things had been different....

Maureen shook herself, refusing to indulge in the game of what if. She loved her life in Cooper's Corner. Leaving New York and her career as a police detective had been easier than she'd imagined. Too bad she couldn't leave all her problems behind, too.

Or rather, one particular problem.

His name was Owen Nevil and he wanted revenge. As a police detective, she'd found enough evidence to send Owen's brother, Carl, to prison for life. Carl had threatened to make her pay for it, reminding her that only one Nevil brother was now behind bars. That threat was the reason she'd left everything behind her and moved to Massachusetts to open Twin Oaks with her brother. She'd had to protect her daughters.

Just the thought of Owen Nevil made a shiver skate up her spine. She was sure he was the one who'd sent the threatening note addressed to her at her old precinct in New York, and now her former boss, Frank Quigg, had alerted her that Owen had skipped parole.

Had he found her? Was he watching Twin Oaks at this moment? Spying on her through the glass?

She stepped away from the window even as she told herself she was being foolish. There was no definite proof that Owen had been responsible for the accident she'd had in the woodshed recently. The roof had simply collapsed from the weight of the snow.

Later she had discovered that the beams had been weakened by something that left gnawing marks. Weakened enough to cause the roof to cave in. But had the marks been made by an animal...or by a man?

She thought back to November, when a stray bullet had just missed Twin Oaks guest Emma Hart before it struck her companion. Emma had been wearing Maureen's coat and scarf at the time. Coincidence? Bad luck? Or was Owen Nevil playing games with her?

The front door opened, making her jump. But it was her brother, carrying in an armload of wood for the fireplace. He kicked the door shut behind him.

"It's freezing out there," he said, dropping his bundle near the hearth, then pulling off his mittens. "I sure hope that groundhog sees his shadow next week. I don't know if I can take six more weeks of winter."

"And I thought you were a tough guy," she teased.

"I am," he assured her. "I just hope all of our guests are warm enough tonight."

"I don't think you have to worry about that," Maureen said dryly. "Some of them seem to be celebrating Valentine's Day early this year. Did I tell you I found one couple necking inside the storage closet this morning?"

Clint reached out and tweaked her hair. "Is that jealousy I hear in your voice, little sister?"

She shook her head. "I'm happily single, thank you very much."

Clint grinned. "You'd still better watch out. It's almost February, which means Cupid will be on the loose. I read somewhere that there's a direct correlation between Valentine's Day and overcrowding in maternity wards nine months later."

His words made Maureen think of Rowena, and her heart contracted for her friend. She knew what it was like to give birth alone. To see the fathers of the other babies making goofy faces outside the nursery window. At least her brother had been there for her.

Clint's grin faded as he studied her expression. "Is something wrong?"

"No, not wrong exactly." She reached up to brush the snowflakes out of his dark hair. "It's Rowena. She's going to have baby."

He looked surprised. "How did this happen?"

She gave him a wry smile. "The usual way."

"I didn't even know she was seeing anyone."

Maureen hesitated. The details of her pregnancy were up to Rowena to tell, especially since it hadn't happened the usual way at all. "It's complicated," she said with a sigh. "I hope it all works out for her."

"It will." Clint assured her. "You've done all right."

"So far," Maureen replied, pushing her worries about Owen Nevil to the back of her mind. She just hoped she could keep them there.

ALAN WALKED into the Twin Oaks Bed and Breakfast late Monday afternoon, the fire blazing in the huge stone hearth a welcome respite from the bitter Massachusetts cold. During the long drive from Toronto he'd wondered what awaited him in Cooper's Corner.

The town looked like the cover of a greeting card, with its quaint buildings and a church with a soaring white steeple. Nestled in the Berkshires, Cooper's Corner seemed like the perfect place to get away from the bustle of the big city. It was obviously a popular destination. He'd only been able to reserve a room at Twin Oaks due to a last-minute cancellation.

Slowly he looked around the large great room, impressed by the simple, cozy elegance of the place. A vintage piano stood in one corner, and the scent of cinnamon lingered in the air.

A man appeared in the doorway that led to a dining room, wiping his large hands on a dish towel. "Can I help you?"

"I'm Alan Rand," he replied, setting down his suitcases. He'd probably overpacked for this trip, but he wasn't certain how long he'd be staying. If he was lucky, he'd be out of Cooper's Corner soon. Or maybe he'd stay on for a while and do some skiing, since he'd made arrangements to work out of the office for the next few weeks. His future plans, both short-term and long-term, all hinged on one woman. "I have a reservation."

"Nice to meet you, Mr. Rand," the man said, flipping the towel over his shoulder and holding out his hand. "I'm Clint Cooper. My sister, Maureen, and I own Twin Oaks."

Alan reached out to shake his hand. "Great place you've got here."

"We like it," Clint said, moving behind the registration desk. He opened the top desk drawer and retrieved a big brass key. "If you'll sign the guest book, I'll be happy to show you up to your room."

After scribbling his signature in the guest book, Alan picked up his suitcases and followed Clint up the staircase. They stopped at the end of the hallway, and Clint pulled the key out of the pocket of his khaki slacks. Then he unlocked the door and swung it open. "This is your room."

Alan walked inside and looked around. The first thing he noticed was another cheery fire crackling in a corner hearth. A bright blue and white quilt covered the four-poster pine bed. But the most spectacular feature of the room was the view of the Berkshires from the large window. Dazzling, snow-covered hills lined with ski trails were framed against the azure blue sky.

"I just took some cookies out of the oven," Clint said, removing a small tin from the nightstand. "I'll fill this up and have my son, Keegan, bring it to you." One corner of his mouth kicked up in a smile. "If you're lucky there'll be a few left by the time he gets here."

"Sounds good," Alan replied, shrugging out of his coat. Clint stood a couple inches taller than he did, at least six-three, and looked like he belonged more in a logging camp than a kitchen. Learning to bake was on Alan's list, but he preferred to handle one challenge at a time.

"There's a breakfast buffet every morning from

seven until nine,'' Clint informed him. ''And a library downstairs if you like to read.''

Alan had a briefcase full of manuscripts to read for work, mostly nonfiction tomes on various technical subjects. It might be nice to do some pleasure reading while he was here. ''Thanks. I'll check it out.''

''Hope you have a pleasant stay here at Twin Oaks.'' Clint moved toward the open door. ''And let me know if there's anything you need.''

''I will.''

By the time Alan had unpacked his suitcases and placed his clothes in the boudoir, a young boy of about twelve appeared in the open doorway with the tin in his hands.

''Here are your cookies.''

''Great. I'm starved.'' Alan took the tin from him, the metal warm against his palms. ''You must be Keegan.''

The boy nodded as Alan popped the lid off the tin. Despite Clint's warning, the tin wasn't empty. It was full of cookies. Their spicy cinnamon aroma teased his nostrils and made his mouth water. ''Hey, snickerdoodles are my favorite.''

''Mine, too,'' Keegan said, still lingering in the doorway. ''They're even better than the chocolate chip ones Dad usually makes.''

Alan held out the tin. ''Want one?''

''Thanks.'' Keegan eagerly reached for a cookie, then downed it in two bites. ''Are you here by yourself?''

Alan nodded. ''Just a short vacation. Actually, I'm

looking for somebody who lives around here. A woman named Rowena Dahl. Do you know her?"

"Sure. She cuts my hair. And she wrote the Christmas Festival play. I was a shepherd."

"She cuts your hair?" Alan asked, a little confused.

"At her barbershop. It's right on Main Street. You probably saw it when you drove here."

He gave a slow nod. "So she's a barber?"

"Yeah. A real good one, too. She even found a way to make Randi and Robin look halfway decent after they cut each other's hair."

Alan didn't know who Randi and Robin were, but at the moment he was too focused on Rowena to ask. The fact that she was a hairdresser set his mind somewhat at ease. His mother and aunt had worked together as hairdressers in Toronto. He found that women who gravitated to that kind of career usually were down-to-earth and warmhearted. Easy to manage. His father had certainly been able to reign over the Rand household with little trouble.

Rowena Dahl was no doubt a simple, unsophisticated countrywoman who would be happy to cooperate with him once she knew all the facts. He was still curious about why she chose to go the route of artificial insemination to conceive a baby. Perhaps Cooper's Corner lacked an abundance of single men. Or maybe Rowena simply wasn't the kind of woman to attract their interest.

The reason didn't really matter. If she was pregnant with his child, then he'd find some way to deal with it that would satisfy them both. Alan was used to handling difficult negotiations with some of the smartest, most sophisticated people in the publishing industry. Rowena Dahl of Cooper's Corner, Massachusetts, would be no problem.

"So how do you know her?" Keegan asked, breaking Alan's reverie.

He blinked. "Who?"

"Rowena."

"Oh." He cleared his throat. "It's…a long story."

Keegan opened his mouth to say something when Clint Cooper's deep voice echoed up the stairway. "Keegan? You up there?"

"Gotta go." The boy turned and headed for the door, grabbing another cookie on his way out. "Do you need anything else, Mr. Rand?"

Alan reached up to run a hand through his short, dark hair. "As a matter of fact, I think I could use a haircut."

CHAPTER THREE

AN HOUR LATER, Alan found himself standing outside the barbershop on Main Street, staring at the closed sign in the leaded glass window of the scarred oak door. The setting sun cast long shadows over the sidewalk as he debated whether to come back tomorrow. The barbershop stood nestled between Tubb's Café and an antique store. The neat brick facade fit nicely among the picturesque storefronts lining both sides of the street. A large, decorative sign that read A Cut Above in bold blue letters hung just under the eaves.

He'd come to Cooper's Corner for the express purpose of discovering whether this Rowena Dahl woman was pregnant with his child. But as he stood here, part of him didn't want to know the answer. He couldn't deny the sudden temptation to turn around and walk away.

But something made him stay.

Alan tugged his overcoat more tightly around him as a gust of bitter wind blew through the street. How had he ever ended up in this mess? It was as if he'd been entered in some kind of bizarre baby lottery. The mother of his child could be anyone. An immature girl of twenty or an older, hardened woman who could hear the incessant ticking of her biological clock. She could be an ex-convict or some kind of religious fanatic. Someone with beliefs and values diametrically opposed to his.

Could Rowena Dahl afford to bring a baby into this world on the salary of a barber? What about her background? Her family? Her love life? The answer to that last question seemed obvious, given her visit to the Orr Fertility Clinic. Or was there another reason?

Ever since he'd discovered a stranger might be carrying his child, his imagination had gone into overdrive. But Alan knew it was time to face reality now—whatever the outcome. A shadow of movement through the glass on the door made his heartbeat quicken. Was it her? Squaring his shoulders, he raised his hand to knock on the door, preparing himself for the worst. But his knuckles rapped only once against the glass before the door opened.

He blinked at the vision standing before him.

The top of her head reached above his chin, which made her at least five foot seven. Her long blond hair hung in silky ringlets almost to her waist. A loose raspberry sweater concealed the upper part of her body, but the black stretch pants she wore revealed a pair of endless legs that made him swallow hard as his gaze slowly moved down the length of her. "Are you Rowena Dahl?"

She smiled and nodded. "You must be from Twin Oaks. Clint called a few minutes ago and told me one of his guests might be stopping by for a haircut."

Her voice carried a hint of smoke that made his gaze travel once again the endless miles of her slender legs, all the way up her luscious body until he met her eyes. They were the color of amethysts, glittering with a warmth that made him feel both hot and cold.

This woman had to go all the way to Toronto for a sperm donor? He was surprised the men of Massachusetts weren't lining up at her door!

He kept staring at her until he saw a tiny wrinkle form on her delicate brow. Then he finally came to his senses and cleared his throat. "I heard you're the best barber in town."

She laughed. "Could it be because I'm the only barber in town? Or hairdresser, for that matter. I bill myself as both, since some of the men around here are more comfortable sitting in a barbershop than a beauty shop."

"I practically grew up in my mother's beauty shop, so that's not a problem for me." Then he pointed to the closed sign hanging on the door. "But it looks like I'm a little late."

She opened the door wider, waving him in. "Not at all. My last appointment of the day just left a little while ago, but I'm always happy to take guests from Twin Oaks."

He stepped inside her shop and was met by the warmth from the radiator against one wall as well as the bright cheeriness of the room. Soft white walls served as the backdrop for a retro decor that featured a checkered blue and white tile floor, two drier chairs upholstered in red and blue gingham fabric and a vintage red Formica counter filled with bottles of shampoo, mousse and styling gel. The shop looked like something he might find in a trendy city salon, not tucked away in a small town like Cooper's Corner.

"I'm Alan," he said, suddenly wondering if the Orr Clinic had released his name to her. "Alan Rand."

But there was no spark of recognition in those unusual eyes. She swiveled the red leather barber chair toward him. "Are you in town for business or pleasure, Mr. Rand?"

"Business," he said curtly, as if he needed to remind himself of that fact. "And please call me Alan."

He shrugged out of his coat and leather gloves, suddenly finding the room almost unbearably hot. He wanted to blame it on the space heater sitting on the floor next to the chair, but he feared the explanation wasn't that simple. He could feel his pulse pick up as he watched her bend over to sweep some hair clippings on the floor into a dustpan.

"Go ahead and have a seat," she said, her back to him. "I'll be with you in a minute."

Alan settled into the barber chair, wondering why he was letting her affect him this way. He'd formed an image of Rowena in his mind—a simple country-woman who might be a little plain, a little shy, perhaps even somewhat repressed.

Instead, he'd found a fantasy woman who could easily grace the cover of the swimsuit edition of *Sports Illustrated* magazine. She wasn't some young bimbette, though. A keen intelligence glittered in her eyes, and he'd guess her age to be close to his—mid-thirties.

Her beauty wasn't artificial, either. She looked as if she didn't have on a trace of makeup. Not that she needed it. Nature had given her long dark lashes and roses in her sculptured cheeks. A perfect nose and lips that were full, pink and inviting.

Alan finally forced himself to look away from her. He couldn't let her distract him like this. The fact that Rowena Dahl was one of the most beautiful women he'd ever met shouldn't make a bit of difference. He was here for one reason and one reason only—to find out if she was pregnant with his baby.

"So what would you like?" she asked, wrapping a blue nylon drape around him and securing the Velcro tab in the back. Then she rested her hands lightly on his shoulders, and he became aware of the subtle scent of gardenias now that she stood close behind him.

He hesitated, suddenly wishing he'd formed some kind of plan before he'd come barging into her shop. He could hardly come right out and ask her if she was pregnant. Better to make small talk and put her at ease. Perhaps she'd even volunteer the information.

"Just a trim," he replied at last, settling back against the chair. She began lightly ruffling his hair with her fingers, and he closed his eyes at the exquisite sensation.

"Do you want to keep the sideburns?"

His eyes flew open. "Yes. No." He sounded like an idiot. "What do you think?"

"I like them," she replied, spritzing his hair with a water bottle. "But since you're a new customer, I want to make sure you're satisfied. You've got nice, thick hair with a slight wave to it."

"That's why I like to keep it short," he confided. "If I let it go too long, it starts to curl."

He sensed rather than saw her smile. "Most people

would consider that a blessing,'' she said. ''At least most of my female customers.''

''I'm not a curls kind of guy.''

''I can see that,'' she said, her voice a little huskier. Then she cleared her throat. ''How about if I take half an inch off the top and back?''

''Sounds good.'' Alan shifted slightly in the chair, reminding himself not to get too comfortable. The haircut wouldn't take long, so he didn't have much time to find out the information he needed.

''So how do you like Twin Oaks?'' she asked, pumping the metal pedal on the chair to raise it.

''Great.'' Alan clenched his jaw in frustration, realizing he should be the one asking the questions.

''Where are you from?''

''Toronto.'' He waited, wondering if that might elicit a reaction. But she just picked up a comb and scissors off the tray in front of her. He ran a finger around the neck edge of the drape. ''Have you been there?''

''Once.'' She ran the comb through his hair, then he heard the crisp clip-clip of the scissors.

''Business or pleasure?'' he asked, repeating her earlier question.

She hesitated. ''I visited a couple of salons while I was there, so I guess you could say a little bit of both.''

His body relaxed under her capable hands. ''Your shop must keep you pretty busy. I bet it's difficult to get away.''

''Yes, but I love being my own boss.''

This obviously wasn't getting him anywhere. How

could he ask Rowena what he really wanted to know. *Are you pregnant with my baby?*

"So how long do you plan to stay in Cooper's Corner?" she asked, bending nearer to carefully cut around his ear.

"I'm not sure. I need a break from the office, but I brought some work along with me."

"What kind of work do you do?"

"I'm in publishing." Alan shifted in his chair with impatience. Why were they talking about *him?*

"Really? I love to read. What kind of books do you publish?"

He realized small talk was one of the tools of her trade, but maybe he could twist the subject to his advantage.

"Nonfiction, mostly," he replied, hastily improvising. "I'm excited about a new book for expectant mothers we're putting out next month. It's from the baby's perspective in the womb. I think it will be a big hit."

"I collect cookbooks," she said without missing a beat. "The oldest one is from eighteen ninety-five. There are some interesting recipes in there, along with remedies for everything from drunkenness to getting struck by lightning." She laughed. "Although, I have to confess I spend more time reading the recipes than actually cooking. I used to live in Manhattan and I'm afraid I got spoiled by take-out dinners."

He wondered if she'd changed the subject from babies to cookbooks on purpose. His comment about expectant mothers hadn't rattled her. On the other hand, why would Rowena share her personal life with a total stranger? Playing games wasn't his style. He'd circled around the subject long enough.

"There you go," she said several minutes later, spinning the chair around so he could see his reflection in the big mirror on the wall. "What do you think?"

He met her gaze in the mirror. "I think it's time for the truth to come out."

Her brow furrowed. "The truth?"

Alan took a deep breath. "I'll tell you why I'm really here if you tell me whether or not you're pregnant with my baby."

A CHILL washed over Rowena as she stared into toffee brown eyes that just a scant moment ago she'd found undeniably sexy. "What?"

He kept his gaze locked on hers in the mirror. "The Orr Fertility Clinic contacted you about their mistake, didn't they? How they inadvertently switched the identification numbers on two of the sperm deposits?"

She didn't answer him, but one hand curled around the comb in her hand until the plastic teeth dug into her palm. Her other hand still held the scissors.

"Unfortunately, my sperm was involved in the mix-up." Alan leaned forward. "So I came to Cooper's Corner to find out if you're pregnant with my baby."

"It's *my* baby," she blurted, realizing too late that she'd answered his question.

Something flickered over his handsome face. Surprise? Disappointment? Resignation? She didn't know the man well enough to tell. She didn't *want* to know him. "I think you should leave."

His eyes narrowed. "I'm not going anywhere until we find a solution to this problem."

Indignation flared inside her. She turned from the mirror and rounded the chair to face him. "The only *problem* I have is with you coming into my shop under false pretenses. So why don't you go back to Toronto and forget any of this ever happened. Forget we ever met. That's certainly what I intend to do."

He slowly shook his head. "It's too late for that. As I said before, I don't plan on going anywhere, Rowena. Not until you answer a few of my questions."

She didn't like his tone. Or his autocratic manner. It reminded her too much of a man from her past. A man who had used any means to manipulate her. "I asked you to leave. Do I have to call the police?"

"Go ahead—if you want our little secret to be all over town."

As much as she hated to admit it, he was right. In a place as small as Cooper's Corner there was a good chance everyone would know everything before morning. It was difficult enough to deal with her pregnancy and the sudden appearance of Alan Rand without having to answer questions from curious neighbors.

She took a deep breath. "What do you want from me?"

He hesitated, his gaze scanning her face. "First, I want you to sit down. You look pale."

She walked on wobbly knees to one of the drier chairs. The last thing she wanted to do was display any weakness around him. Especially when he seemed so coolly confident. Why hadn't she noticed that air of command before? Probably because she was too busy trying not to drool over him. Despite his sneaky tactics, she had to admit Alan Rand was a handsome man. At least six foot one and most of it muscle.

But she'd dealt with a man like him six years ago when she lived in New York—and knew how easily a handsome face could hide a cold heart.

"Do you have any proof to back up your claim?" she asked, feeling stronger. "It could be anyone...."

He shook his head. "Not anyone. I'm the father of your baby, Rowena."

"So why didn't you tell me right away? Why all the subterfuge?"

"I knew you went to the Orr Fertility Clinic for the insemination procedure, but I didn't have any proof that it was a success. So I had to find out for myself."

Success didn't seem like the right word to describe the current chaos in her life. Almost four months pregnant with the baby of a stranger. Too many sleepless nights since learning about the actions of the Orr Fertility Clinic. And now this.

"You didn't have to come all the way to Cooper's Corner," she said, trying to keep her voice calm and even. She'd let him upset her enough already. "You could have just called me and asked your questions over the telephone."

He lifted a skeptical brow. "And give you a chance to run away?"

Her jaw tightened. "I hate to disappoint you, Alan, but I don't scare that easily. Even if this is your baby, you don't have any claim to it. I was told at the Orr Clinic that all sperm donors are required to sign a release relinquishing parental rights."

''That may be true,'' he countered. ''But I never signed a release because I never intended my sperm to be donated to anyone.''

''Then why did you go there in the first place?''

''Personal reasons,'' he said in a clipped voice. ''Why did you go there, Rowena? You're a beautiful woman. Wouldn't it have been easier to just bring a sperm donor home for the night instead of traveling all the way to Toronto?''

Of all the nerve. ''Personal reasons,'' she said, echoing his response. ''And I'm not ready to accept the fact that you are the father of this baby. I want proof.''

He arched a dark brow. ''What kind of proof?''

''I don't know,'' she exclaimed, wishing her head would stop spinning. Just a few moments ago they'd been chatting about books and the curl in his hair. ''Something that proves you're the father of my baby. Like a paternity test.''

''No problem.'' He reached for his wallet, then pulled out a business card and handed it to her. ''My cellular phone number is on there, so you can reach me anytime, day or night. I'll take the test whenever and wherever you want.''

''How about Siberia?'' she quipped, pocketing the card without looking at it.

He gave her a tight smile. ''That would only delay the inevitable. For now, I think you should assume that I am the father.''

She shook her head, tilting her chin up a notch. ''I don't think either one of us should assume anything. Especially since we already know the Orr Fertility

Clinic is prone to making mistakes. The father of my baby could be anyone.''

He arched a dark brow. "And you take comfort in that thought?"

She tried not to flinch, but he'd hit a nerve. Despite her shock at finding the father of her baby in her barbershop, she couldn't deny that part of her was relieved to finally know his identity. But at what cost? At least an anonymous sperm donor meant no one could interfere in her life. No one could force her child to go through the emotional torment she'd endured while growing up.

Alan didn't say anything, just stood there watching her. She met his gaze, determined not to look away. He seemed formidable, but he must have a weakness somewhere. Everyone did. Could she find it? And if she did, would she have the nerve to use it to her advantage? Even for the sake of her baby?

"There is another possibility I didn't consider," he said at last, his gaze moving over her in a way that brought a hot blush to her cheeks.

"What?"

He cleared his throat. "I realize this is none of my business, but if you were involved with another man last autumn…" He let his voice trail off, his meaning clear to both of them.

She considered lying, but somehow she knew Alan still wouldn't back off. If she claimed to be in a relationship, he'd have even more questions about why she went to the clinic for the insemination procedure, and the truth would eventually come out anyway. "There is no man in my life."

He nodded, his face grim. "Then I am the father."

"Maybe," she replied. "I think it would be better to wait until we receive the test results. If you're not the father, then we have nothing to talk about."

He shook his head. "I've learned the hard way that it's better to face bad news and deal with it head-on. Believe me, Rowena, I'm not any happier about this situation than you are. I'm sure as hell not ready to be a father. But I know we can find a solution to our problem."

Problem. It was the second time he'd used that word, and it raked against her nerves like fingernails on a chalkboard. How dare he come here and lay claim to her baby. A baby he obviously didn't want. A fierce protectiveness enveloped her, shaking her to the very core. She loved this baby. And she'd do anything to protect it. "Exactly how do you intend to do that?"

"I know neither one of us is happy about this situation," he began. "But I'm hoping we can come to some kind of understanding that will satisfy us both."

"I'd be ecstatic if you'd just go back to Toronto."

"I will as soon as we settle this matter." He reached into the front of his jacket. "You're about four months along, right?"

"Right," she replied, his words making her a little uneasy. Why did he care how far along she was? And why the hell was he pulling out his checkbook?

"I know a good doctor you can go to in Williamstown," he continued. "I'm willing to pay all expenses, along with a little extra for all your trouble."

Trouble. That was definitely the right word to describe Alan Rand. Along with condescending, over-bearing and conceited. She hoped those traits weren't hereditary.

"That isn't necessary," she said tightly.

"I insist." He flipped open his checkbook. "I'll write you a check right now to cover the initial expenses."

Apprehension filled her. He'd told her he wasn't ready to be a father. But did he actually intend to bribe her into making that a reality?

Rowena sat back in the chair and watched as he pulled a silver pen out of his pocket, then scribbled out an amount. He'd obviously assumed from her job at the barbershop that she didn't have much money. Her anger ebbed, temporarily overridden by a sort of morbid fascination. She wondered what the going rate for getting rid of a *problem* was these days.

"Here you go," he said, holding the check out to her.

She stood to take it from him, looking at the amount. The number of zeroes in it impressed her.

"As you can see, I'm willing to pay my fair share," he said.

"That won't be necessary." She ripped the check in half, then tore it again.

"What are you doing?" Alan exclaimed, his brow furrowed in confusion.

She let the pieces flutter to the floor. "Turning down your generous offer."

"You want more money?" he exclaimed.

She rose to her feet, her protective instincts coming on full force. "No. I don't want anything from you. I don't need your money, Alan. No amount of money could make me even consider terminating this pregnancy."

His eyes widened. "Wait a minute," he interjected, holding up both hands. "You don't understand...."

But she wasn't about to let him bully her anymore. She'd learned the hard way that it only gave men like this a greater license to harass.

Rowena advanced on him and saw his glance fall to the scissors she still held in her hands. "I think it's time for you to leave now."

"Let's be rational," he said, backing toward the door.

"I'm not feeling too rational at the moment," she replied, still advancing. He was a big man, but he'd threatened her child and he'd awakened some primitive instinct inside her that wouldn't be denied.

"You're making a mistake," he said, tripping over the threshold as he stumbled out the door.

"You're the one who made the mistake, Mr. Rand," she said, one hand gripping the edge of the door. "I want this baby and I intend to keep this baby. Even if its father's gene pool could have used some chlorinating!"

Then she slammed the door in his face.

CHAPTER FOUR

HE'D BLOWN IT.

Alan stared at the door of the barbershop, tempted to pound on it until she let him back inside. But he knew Rowena was too furious at the moment to listen to reason. He shook his head as he turned and headed for his car. Alan had intended to make a show of good faith with that check and his recommendation of a respected obstetrician. Instead, she believed he wanted her to terminate the pregnancy.

"Mr. Charming strikes again," he muttered, his breath coming out in frosty puffs of air as he slid behind the wheel of his Ford Mustang. He replayed their conversation over in his mind as he drove to Twin Oaks, wincing when he remembered some of the things he'd said. What the hell had gotten into him?

But he knew the answer. *Rowena.* His tongue had started turning somersaults the moment he'd laid eyes on her. Hell, he could hardly think straight around her, much less negotiate their touchy situation. So instead of telling her he simply wanted to be a father to their baby, he'd come on like some big shot and tried to buy her compliance.

Big mistake.

One he definitely needed to rectify. The only question was how. From the sparks he'd seen in those amethyst eyes, she'd rather stab him with her scissors than speak to him again. He'd gone into that barbershop expecting to find a woman he could impress with his stature and big-city sophistication. But he'd severely underestimated her. Rowena Dahl was a mature, intelligent, witty woman. And as much as he hated to admit it, he found those traits even more seductive than her beautiful face and luscious figure.

Alan parked outside Twin Oaks Bed and Breakfast, then walked up the path lit by a pair of wrought-iron carriage lamps. Once inside, he ignored the amorous couples gathered around the crackling blaze in the huge stone fireplace and took the stairs two at a time to his room. He had his cellular phone out before the door closed behind him. He dialed Brad's number, then swore softly when he heard the busy signal buzzing in his ear.

A father. He was going to be a father. The shock of it still unnerved him. This wasn't the way Alan had planned it. He wanted a family—someday. But in the traditional way. With a wife. A big house somewhere in the suburbs of Toronto. Perhaps, if he ever learned to swim, even a cabin up at Lake Temagami—like the Haleys.

Alan redialed his lawyer's phone number, only to hear a busy signal again. He carried the cell phone to the window and looked into the black, starless night. Tiny lights dotted the ski slopes, outlining the runs. He could teach his child to ski. Sign him up for a hockey team. Or her, if it was a girl. As the reality slowly sank in, he realized there was so much he wanted to do.

If he was given the chance.

He turned away from the window and walked to the hearth, bending to place another log on the fire. A few moments later, a blaze flared up and Alan held out his hands to warm them. The flames reminded him of the amethyst fire he'd seen in Rowena's eyes when she'd torn up his check.

Damn, she was beautiful.

That was his first mistake. He'd let his attraction to her distract him from his goal. Something he couldn't afford to let happen again. Alan needed to focus on what really mattered—the baby. He might have screwed up tonight, but that didn't mean he was going to turn tail and meekly back down from his rights as a father.

Taking a seat by the fireplace, he dialed Brad's home number for a third time, gratified when he finally heard it ringing.

A deep male voice sounded on the other end of the line. "Hello?"

"I found Rowena Dahl," Alan said without preamble. "She is pregnant."

Brad breathed a long sigh over the line. "So what is she like?"

A hellcat who could rip out a man's heart with one glance. "Let's just say she's not at all what I expected."

"Is that good or bad?"

Good question. "I'm not sure."

"Do you still want to pursue your rights as the father of this baby?"

"Absolutely."

"It won't be easy," Brad informed him. "Especially with you a Canadian citizen and Rowena living in the United States. I'm not even sure which country would have jurisdiction over the case."

"I don't care how difficult it is or how expensive," Alan said firmly. "I have to do this, Brad. I intend to be part of my baby's life."

Brad didn't need to ask him why. As a child, Alan had once overheard the Haleys refer to George Rand as the invisible man. Maybe that's why they'd gone out of their way to make Alan feel like a part of their family. Inviting him to spend a week with them at Lake Temagami and trying to help him overcome his fear of water. His father might not care about him, but Bradford Haley, Sr., had shown him the way a good father should act. The way Alan intended to care for his child.

"Okay," Brad said, resignation in his voice. "How do you want to handle this?"

"I want to be the one to make the first move," Alan replied. "Catch her off guard."

"I can do that, but these kind of fertility cases are new and messy. It could literally take years, Alan. Are you sure this can't be settled amicably between you?"

His mind flashed to her slamming the door in his face. "Positive. I didn't handle it well."

"Do you want liberal visitation with the baby?"

"Yes. Full summers and at least every other weekend.'' He hesitated. "Any chance I could share joint custody?''

Brad whistled low. "That might be a tough one. I won't sugarcoat it, Alan. A mother's rights have traditionally trumped a father's in past court cases. Unless you have something we can use that would make joint custody appear to be in the best interests of the child.''

"Like what?''

"Anything that casts a questionable light on her character. That means we'd have to start digging into her past. Like I said before—it could get messy.''

Alan rubbed the bridge of his nose between his fingers. It was already messy. His confrontation with Rowena tonight had left him unsettled and strangely restless. "I don't want to do that. But what choice do I have? She wants me to just walk away.''

"You still might want to consider it, Alan. I understand how you feel, but as your lawyer I have to tell you that this isn't going to be an easy fight. It will cost money. Time. Custody battles are never fun.''

"I'm not looking for fun,'' he retorted. "I'm fighting for my child. And I don't care how much time or money it takes. I won't stop until I win.''

EARLY THE NEXT morning, Rowena sat in her lawyer's office in New Ashford, her fingers twisting together in her lap. She hadn't slept at all last night, her imagination too busy concocting the many ways that Alan Rand could screw up her baby's life.

Now she prattled off those fears to Bobby Claymore, an older man with silver hair and a neatly trimmed goatee. Originally from Montana, he wore a black string tie, a crisp white shirt and a pair of snakeskin cowboy boots. But his gentle cowboy persona had led more than one courtroom opponent to underestimate him.

At last Bobby held up both hands to stop her in midsentence. "Whoa, there. I know you're upset, Rowena, but take a deep breath. That's right. Now slow down and let's start over from the beginning."

Rowena gave him a shaky nod, furious with Alan Rand for causing this turmoil in her life. Why did she let the man affect her this way? "I'm sorry. I've never been in a situation like this before."

"I understand," Bobby replied, then swiveled in his chair to pull a file off the shelf behind him. "I did some research when you called last week asking me to contact the Orr Fertility Clinic about their error. But it seems there's just not much precedence for this kind of case."

"I'm not interested in filing a lawsuit," she clarified. "I want to know how to get this man out of my life."

He opened the file. "Tell me again why you chose the Orr Clinic for this procedure."

"My doctor recommended it," she explained. "The Orr Clinic has a new procedure designed especially for women over thirty-five who have difficulty conceiving. When my trip to the Reproductive Center in New York was unsuccessful, he told me about the positive results they were having in Toronto. The Orr Clinic sent me a catalog of sperm donor profiles before the procedure, and I mailed back a form with my choice.''

"Which brings us to our current situation."

She nodded. "A man showed up in my shop yesterday claiming to be the father of my baby. He said his sperm deposit at the Orr Fertility Clinic was never intended to be a donation. He also claimed he didn't sign a release of his parental rights, either. Then he offered me a check to take care of the—'' her fingers made quotation marks in the air to emphasize the last word ''—*problem.*''

Bobby leaned back in his chair. "Did he threaten you in any way when he asked you to terminate the pregnancy?''

"No," she said slowly. "In fact, he never actually came out and told me that's what he wanted me to do. I just assumed that's what he meant. Can I get a restraining order against him to keep him out of my life?''

"I'm afraid it might be more complicated than that." Bobby took off his glasses and wiped the lenses with a tissue. "If this man wants you to terminate the pregnancy, then he doesn't have a legal leg to stand on. But if he wants more…''

"More?" Rowena echoed, trepidation filling her.

Bobby hesitated. "I'm intrigued by the fact he came to Cooper's Corner in person to find you.''

"I told you," she said. "He wanted to discover if I was pregnant.''

Her attorney nodded. "I know. But he could have accomplished that any number of ways. The fact remains that if he is the biological father of your baby, he's already taking a proactive role. If the pregnancy continues, he might want to assert his rights as a parent.''

She blinked. ''Can he do that?''

''He'll have to go to court and prove paternity first. Of course, that's only the beginning. Just establishing jurisdiction will be a lengthy process.''

''He's already agreed to a paternity test,'' Rowena told him. ''I called my doctor last night to set it up. But he said the only way we can conduct a paternity test before the baby is born is if I undergo an amniocentesis. That isn't possible until the fifth month, and even then it carries some risks.''

''Risks you aren't willing to take,'' Bobby ventured.

''That's right.''

''So it's possible we won't know if Mr. Rand is the father until after the baby's birth. When is your due date, by the way?''

''In early July.'' She licked dry lips. ''But I don't want Alan Rand's shadow hanging over us for the next five months.''

''If Mr. Rand is the father,'' Bobby mused, ''you should be able to collect child support payments.''

She shook her head. ''I don't want his money or anything else from him. My parents divorced when I was four years old. I lost count of the number of times they took each other to court over support payments and visitation rights.''

Compassion shone in Bobby's faded brown eyes. ''I understand. Unfortunately, I've seen it happen too many times. How can parents be so blind to the fact that the one they're hurting the most is their own child?''

Rowena knew her pregnancy hormones had kicked in when his words brought a flood of memories washing down on her. She usually kept her past to herself, but he needed to know how important protecting this baby from a nasty, prolonged custody suit was to her.

''I know exactly what you mean,'' she replied. ''I became a weapon my parents could use against each other. My father would give me presents for my birthday and Christmas that he knew my mother didn't approve of for a little girl. And she would plan these exotic vacations for the two of us during the summer, then lay the blame on him if I couldn't go because of the visitation order.''

Bobby didn't murmur sympathetic platitudes, he just sat back in his chair and listened to her.

''Their tug-of-war kept on escalating as I was growing up. One time my father was late bringing me home from a weekend visit with him, and my mother called the police. He never forgave her for that, and from that day on he would circle the block around the house each time he brought me home, trying to make her worry that he'd really done it. One time we circled the same block for an hour.''

Bobby shook his head, and she knew that as a family lawyer, he'd probably heard worse.

''They got so caught up in their battle with each other,'' she continued, ''that they had no idea what it was doing to me. The odd thing was that I knew they both really did love me.''

''Damn strange way of showing it,'' he said at last.

"I know," she replied with a shadow of a smile. "Sometimes I think that's what made it so hard. When I was a teenager, I started to dread the holidays. I knew my parents would make me choose who I wanted to spend them with, and I'd tear myself up with guilt trying to decide who I would hurt the least with my choice. I was determined to make them both happy while they were equally determined to make each other miserable. They loved me, but they hated each other more."

"Is it any better now that you're an adult?"

She nodded. "Yes, but I hardly see them anymore. They both remarried. My father lives in California, and my mother moved to Brazil with her husband, who has a business there. In some ways I feel as alone as I did growing up."

His brown eyes twinkled. "Well, you won't be alone much longer."

"I know," she said, love for her baby welling up inside her. "But I never want my child to go through what I did. If Alan Rand is the biological father and pursues visitation rights, my baby's life will be in chaos—shuttled back and forth across the border of two countries for the next eighteen years."

A gentle knock sounded on the door, then it opened and Bobby Claymore's secretary stole in silently to place a stack of mail on his desk.

"Thanks, Hildy," he murmured before she closed the door behind her. He gave the stack of envelopes a quick glance, then pulled one from the middle. "Looks like that paternity test might not be necessary."

Her heart skipped a beat. "What do you mean?"

He flipped the envelope around so she could see the Orr Fertility Clinic emblem in the corner. "It seems the clinic has finally decided to respond to my inquiries."

She held her breath as he reached for the letter opener and neatly slit the envelope open. His gaze quickly scanned the letter, then he handed it to her.

Rowena looked down and saw the name of the sperm donor in black and white—Alan Rand. She fell back against the chair. "So he is the father."

Bobby leaned forward to take the letter from her hands, then perused it slowly. "According to the Orr Clinic, the sperm donor identity number you selected was transcribed incorrectly. There is supposed to be a method in place to double-check the donor number before the insemination procedure, but apparently somebody screwed up along the way."

She closed her eyes, remembering her initial relief at discovering the mysterious sperm donor's identity. Alan Rand fit none of the nightmare scenarios she'd imagined, yet he was creating an entirely new nightmare for her.

"Are you sure you don't want to sue the Orr Clinic?" Bobby asked, his brown eyes lit with indignation.

She shook her head. "I don't need their money. I'm not interested in child support payments from Alan Rand, either. All I want is for him to leave me and my baby alone."

He sighed. "I understand. But I think we should

prepare for the possibility that Mr. Rand might take you to court to assert his rights as the father.''

"But it's *my* baby," she countered, feeling as if everything in her life was slipping out of control. "Alan Rand didn't even know my name until the truth about the clinic's error came out.''

"That's the problem," Bobby replied, slipping his bifocals into his shirt pocket. "According to what you told me, Mr. Rand never signed away his rights to the disposition of his sperm. That means he may very well have a case for pursuing visitation rights, although it will be up to the courts to decide.''

She clung to that kernel of hope. "So it's possible a judge might deny Alan those rights and make him leave us alone?''

"Possibly," Bobby agreed, but looked doubtful. "The outcome of custody cases is always hard to predict, especially with the proliferation of unusual ones involving new technologies like frozen embryos and in-vitro fertilization. The courts are bogged down with them.''

She slumped back in the chair. "This is a nightmare.''

He leaned forward. "Look, Rowena, I'll be straight with you—this case could be one big mess. But if you're right about Mr. Rand wanting you to terminate the pregnancy, then he may have no interest in this child. You may never see him again.''

If only she could be so lucky. "And if I'm wrong?''

He sighed. "Then we'll give him the toughest fight of his life. But let's just take it one step at a time. You go on home now and try not to worry.''

That was like telling her not to breathe. She stood up. "Thank you, Bobby. I really appreciate you squeezing me in this morning."

He smiled as he rose to his feet and escorted her to the door. "No problem. I hope we can resolve this situation to your satisfaction."

Rowena could only nod, her throat tight as she left his office. Her attorney hadn't given her the reassurances she so desperately wanted. Anything could happen if this case went into the court system.

No matter what she had to do, Rowena couldn't let that happen. Tears she'd kept at bay since last evening spilled onto her cheeks. She ducked into her car before the tears could freeze on her skin. Then she drove out of New Ashford, skipping her usual stops at her favorite antique shops.

Rowena had never battled with anyone quite like Alan before. Her hands tightened on the steering wheel as she pulled onto the highway leading to Cooper's Corner. One thing was certain.

Alan Rand was in for the fight of his life.

CHAPTER FIVE

ALAN WALKED carefully down the wide oak staircase Tuesday morning, his head on the verge of exploding. He'd made the mistake of indulging in too many hot buttered rums in his room last night after talking to his lawyer.

The liquor had hit him especially hard since he'd given up drinking after his diagnosis three years ago. He'd given up butter, too.

Adopting a healthy lifestyle had been on his list, and he'd rigorously stuck to a low-cholesterol diet that included almost no alcohol. Some of his friends and colleagues thought Alan had gone a bit overboard on his health kick, but then they hadn't been blindsided by one of the scariest diseases on the planet.

He hadn't been worried about his diet last night, though. The only thing he could think about was Rowena Dahl. It had been a very long time since he'd found a woman so stubborn. So intriguing. So damn frustrating. He still couldn't believe the way she'd kicked him out of her shop—or that he'd let her do it.

So why was he the one who felt guilty this morning?

Of course, that guilt was overshadowed by a pounding head, a desert-dry mouth and a queasy stomach. When he first woke up, he'd been tempted to pull the pillow over his head and die in peace. Then Alan remembered the baby and knew he had to live through this hangover from hell. Even more important, he needed to find some way to deal with Rowena Dahl.

As he entered the dining room, the savory aromas emanating from the serving bar almost made him turn right around and head to his room. Steeling himself against a tidal wave of nausea, he walked into the room and surveyed the wide variety of dishes lined up on the buffet. Steam rose from the platters of ham, bacon and sausage—all foods guaranteed to upset his sensitive stomach. At last he helped himself to a small glass of fresh squeezed orange juice and a toasted English muffin.

"Good morning, Mr. Rand," Keegan said, seated in front of a plate piled high with walnut griddle cakes, scrambled eggs and several links of sausages. The boy ate with a gusto that was at odds with his lanky body.

"Morning," Alan mumbled, averting his gaze from Keegan's plate. There were several empty chairs around the enormous mahogany table. He took the one farthest from the sight of those sausages.

"My dad's in the kitchen making some more griddle cakes," Keegan said, reaching for the container of maple syrup and slathering the thick, amber syrup over everything on his plate. Then he looked at Alan's plate with a puzzled frown. "Did someone forget to tell you the breakfast buffet is all you can eat?"

"This is all I can manage today," Alan replied,

reaching for the orange juice. He took a tentative sip, pleasantly surprised when it went down smoothly. It revived him enough to spread some honey on his toasted English muffin before he took a bite.

"Okay," the boy replied. "But you can go back for seconds and thirds if you want."

"Thanks."

The door between the kitchen and dining room swung open, and Clint walked out carrying a platter of steaming griddle cakes. Alan looked between father and son, noting they shared the same dark hair and green eyes. And obviously the same love for walnut griddle cakes.

An older man followed Clint, slightly stooped and rawboned, with gray peppering his black hair. He wore faded denim overalls and a worn, long-sleeved cotton shirt, both of which hung on his thin frame.

"Go ahead and help yourself, Ed," Clint said to the man as he added the griddle cakes to the buffet. "And take that last raspberry muffin if you'd like. I've got more baking in the oven."

Ed slowly shuffled toward the buffet and picked up a plate. "You sure you have enough food, Clint? I'd hate for your guests to go hungry."

"We've always got more than enough," Clint assured him. "In fact, you'll be doing us a favor by helping us get rid of some of this food." He indicated all the empty chairs in the dining room. "We're full up with couples through Valentine's Day. Seems most of them are finding a reason to skip breakfast."

"That's so dumb," Keegan said, digging into his

waffle cakes. "Why would they want to stay in bed and miss breakfast?"

The three men looked at one another, but didn't say anything.

Ed sat down next to Alan, then frowned at Alan's plate. "Don't you like eggs, son?"

Clint grinned as he took the chair beside his son. "Ed Taylor raises chickens and supplies us with fresh eggs every week. He's an expert on the subject of poultry."

Alan's stomach rebelled at the thought of ingesting any of the fluffy scrambled eggs on the buffet. "I'm not a big breakfast eater."

Ed shook his head, then turned into his own breakfast. "Eggs are nature's perfect food. Did you know they provide all the essential vitamins and minerals we need?"

Keegan brightened. "So that means I can eat eggs instead of vegetables?"

"Good try," Clint said with a smile. "But I think you can handle both."

Ed nodded. "Your father's right, Keegan. Moderation in all things is best. Of course, all that cholesterol malarkey in the news scared a bunch of people off eggs. But I've been eating them for over five decades, and there's nothing much wrong with me."

Alan smiled to himself, deciding it probably wasn't a good idea to share the low-cholesterol diet tips he'd learned with Ed.

The men all looked up as a tall woman with long chestnut hair entered the dining room. Two little girls followed her, both slightly chubby with identical faces and hair the same color as their mother's. One of the little girls looked at Alan and whispered something to her sister. Then they both stared at him with big blue-green eyes.

"Good morning, everyone," the woman said brightly.

"You three came just in the nick of time," Clint said. "Keegan was about to finish off the last of the griddle cakes."

"The girls and I decided to sleep late this morning," she explained, pulling out chairs for her daughters.

Clint stood up to make the introductions. "Alan, this is my sister, Maureen, and her daughters, Randi and Robin. Maureen, this is the guest I was telling you about—Alan Rand from Toronto."

"Nice to meet you," Maureen said, reaching out to shake his hand. To Alan's surprise, her grip was almost as firm as her brother's.

Then she turned to Ed, placing a hand on his thin shoulder. "This is such a nice surprise. I'm so glad you could join us for breakfast today, Ed."

"Clint wouldn't take no for an answer," Ed replied, looking a little sheepish.

"Good for him. I hope you know you're welcome here anytime." Then Maureen turned to bestow a teasing smile on Keegan. "And I hope *you* saved some griddle cakes for your cousins."

"Just make sure they save some for me," Keegan replied, casting a worried glance at the buffet as Maureen began to fill the twins' plates.

Alan watched the little girls, wondering what it

would be like if he had a daughter. Would she be a blonde like Rowena or have his dark hair? He hoped she inherited Rowena's unusual amethyst eyes. Then again, Rowena might be carrying his son. A boy he could teach to camp and fish, just as Mr. Haley had taught him.

Maureen sat next to Ed. "I can't believe you passed up Clint's cinnamon rolls, Ed Taylor. What happened to your sweet tooth?"

"Oh, now don't you worry, Maureen. I've still got it," Ed replied with a chuckle. "I'll be having a couple of those cinnamon rolls for dessert."

Randi Cooper giggled behind her hand. "You can't have dessert at breakfast!"

"You certainly can, young lady," Ed countered, a twinkle in his warm brown eyes. "Why, I used to make dessert for my little girl, Jennifer, every morning when she was growing up." He shook a bony finger in the air. "But only if she ate all her eggs."

"Why?" Robin asked.

"Because eggs are the very best way to start the day," Ed replied.

Randi pointed one tiny finger toward Alan's plate. "But he's not eating eggs."

Maureen gently pulled her daughter's hand back. "You just pay attention to your own plate, young lady."

"Okay, Mom," Randi said with a shy smile as she picked up her fork.

"Mr. Rand knows Rowena." Keegan piped up as if trying to distract attention from his cousin. It worked. Everyone at the table turned to stare at Alan.

"You do?" Clint asked.

"Well, not really." He hedged, wondering how he could possibly explain the situation. "We only actually met in person yesterday."

"Oh," Maureen replied. "Then how do you know her? Are you an old fan of *Another Dawn*?"

He blinked, thoroughly confused by her question. *Another Dawn* was the long-running soap opera his mother had watched religiously every day while he was growing up. "I've seen it a few times."

"What's *Another Dawn*?" Ed asked as he picked up a knife to cut his sausages.

"It's one of those soap operas that's on in the afternoon," Clint replied, scooping up a forkful of scrambled eggs. "Rowena Dahl used to play one of the lead characters. She was a big star on the show until about six years ago when they killed off her character."

Alan's mouth fell open. He quickly closed it again, then he looked at his plate. Rowena was a soap opera star? His Rowena? But why was he surprised? She had the face and body to be a star. He wondered if his mother had seen Rowena on the show. And if she had liked her. Part of him really hoped she had.

"They killed her?" Randi echoed, a worried frown creasing her forehead.

"It's just pretend," Keegan reassured her. "Rowena's okay."

"That's right, honey," Maureen said, leaning over to give her daughter a reassuring hug.

Alan didn't say anything, still trying to absorb the full impact of what he'd just heard. The mother of his baby was a former television star. Every time he thought he had Rowena figured out, something about her surprised him. Now he had more questions than ever. Why was a former actress working as a barber? How long had Rowena been in show business? And why had she left?

"I can't believe I never heard this before," Ed said, shaking his head in wonder. "Has she been trying to keep it a secret?"

"I don't think so," Clint replied. "I first heard about it when I moved to town. Anyone who watched the show would know about it."

"Her character's name was Savannah Corrington," Maureen added, helping one of the twins butter a piece of toast. "I heard they revived the role recently with a new actress. One of those miracle resurrections that are so popular on soap operas."

It was Keegan's turn to look puzzled. "Why didn't they use Rowena for the part? She starred in the Christmas Festival play this year and she was really good."

Maureen shrugged. "I don't know the particulars, but I'm not really surprised she's staying in Cooper's Corner. She likes it here so much that I don't think she'll ever want to leave."

"Lucky for us," Clint added, ruffling one of the twins' hair, "since she gives the best haircut around."

"I sure wish I could have seen her on that show," Ed said, leaning back in his chair. "Afraid the chicken ranch keeps me too busy to watch much television."

"Well, it's not too late, Ed." Maureen reached over to cut one of the twins' griddle cakes into small pieces. "The library's got the full archives of videotapes from the years Rowena was on *Another Dawn,* as well as several old copies of *Soap Opera Digest* with articles about her."

Ed nodded. "I may have to check those out. Clint's right. She sure gives a darn good haircut."

Alan intended to do the same. Even though he knew those soap opera magazines were usually full of gossip, maybe he could learn something valuable about Rowena. He was more curious about her than ever.

Then again, he had people at this table who knew Rowena personally. Maybe they could give him some insight into the mother of his baby. Something he could use to his advantage so she wouldn't view him as the enemy.

When Maureen and Clint began discussing Twin Oaks business, Alan turned to the man beside him. "So is Rowena your regular barber, Ed?"

The older man nodded. "The heck of it is that I'm paying more money for a haircut now than I did ten years ago and I have less hair!"

"That hardly seems fair."

He sighed. "Well, that seems to be the way with everything these days. I went grocery shopping last week, and a pound of bananas cost me over two dollars. And don't even get me started on the price of automobiles."

"The price of cars has skyrocketed since I was a kid," Alan agreed.

"It's outrageous what some folks charge," Ed said indignantly. "Pure and simple greed. The price of eggs hasn't gone up in years. That's why I'm still driving a twenty-five-year-old pickup truck.''

"I wonder why she gave up acting," Alan said, steering the conversation to Rowena. "It must be hard to leave the limelight."

"Maybe so." Ed shrugged his thin shoulders. "I can't say I blame her for wanting to leave New York, though. Big cities have never appealed to me."

"Does she have any family around here?"

Ed paused to think a moment, his fork poised in midair. "I don't think so. Never heard her mention anybody. How about you, Alan? Cooper's Corner is a long way from Toronto. Are you visiting family or friends around here?"

"No." He didn't bother to mention that his father lived in Albany, only a couple of hours away. But given their almost nonexistent relationship, George Rand might as well live half a world away. "I'm here on vacation."

"Well, you're more than welcome to stop by the chicken ranch. 'Course, it's nothing fancy, but we've got plenty of good sight-seeing around here. Smith's Maple Sugar Bush is close by and has a one-hundred-year-old working sugarhouse. I'd be glad to show you if you'd like to take a tour."

The only sight he wanted to see was Rowena. But what could it hurt to tour the area? Especially if his child might grow up here. "Thanks, Ed. I think I'll take you up on it."

"Good enough," Ed said, visibly pleased. "Lots of antique shops around here, too, if you're interested."

Alan shook his head. "I'm not a collector."

"Me, neither." Ed chuckled. "I suppose I've got plenty of antiques out at my place, too, but I've just always called 'em junk."

"Rowena seems to like them," Alan said, finding himself unable to stop thinking about her. "Her shop had a lot of vintage fixtures. It looks great."

"I've seen her at a couple of estate auctions," Ed concurred as he salted his eggs. "Those are really the best places to get a good buy if you're into antiques. Some people even make a hobby of it."

"Does she go alone?" Alan asked, still perplexed that a woman like her wasn't involved with anyone.

Ed shrugged. "I guess so."

Alan didn't understand how a woman like Rowena could be unattached. Of course, he could ask the same of himself. Ever since he'd beaten cancer, his life had been full of activities. Almost too full to have any kind of a social life. But none of those activities could seem to assuage the aching emptiness he sometimes felt inside.

In the last three years, he'd dated only a handful of women. And no one more than once or twice. The playboy life had never appealed to him, but now more than ever he wanted something other than a temporary relationship. Something that had meaning. Purpose. Something he couldn't seem to find, no matter how hard he tried.

"I wonder if Rowena ever gets lonely," he mused.

"Rowena?" Ed said, loudly enough to draw the attention of Clint and Maureen. "Heck, no. She doesn't seem lonely to me. Always so sweet and cheerful."

Maureen spoke up. "Ed's right. Rowena has plenty of good friends to watch out for her."

The woman's tone was friendly enough, but Alan heard the note of warning behind it. No doubt she wondered why he was so interested in Rowena Dahl.

"I'm glad to hear it," Alan said, realizing it was time to change the subject. He'd already made an enemy of Rowena. He didn't want to alienate anybody else in Cooper's Corner. "By the way, I may need to send some work to my office in Toronto while I'm here. Do you happen to have a fax machine available?"

Clint nodded. "I have one in the office you're welcome to use anytime."

"Thanks," Alan said, rising from his chair and dropping his linen napkin on his plate. "And thanks for breakfast, too. It was great."

"You're welcome," Maureen said, her gaze friendly once more. "Please let us know if you need anything else. And don't forget to come down for afternoon tea. We serve around four o'clock."

"Thanks," he replied, pushing his chair in. "I'll be sure to do that."

Alan walked out of the dining room and up the stairs to his bedroom. At least his head wasn't pounding anymore. A low ache in his temple made him grab a couple of aspirins out of his suitcase and wash them down with a glass of water. Now if he could just get this fascination with Rowena Dahl out of his system.

Somehow he knew the cure wouldn't be so easy.

CHAPTER SIX

ROWENA WALKED into Cooper's Corner General Store two days after her consultation with her attorney and stomped her snowy boots on the large rubber mat. The heat emanating from the radiator melted the icy snow-flakes clinging to her hair and eyelashes.

Phyllis Cooper, a short, portly woman with gray-blond hair, stood behind the cash register. She and her husband, Philo, owned the store and took an active interest in all of their customers. Sometimes too active. The couple were known for sharing the latest news and juicy tidbits with everyone who walked into their store. But they were good people at heart.

"Think this dang snow will stop anytime soon?" Phyllis asked her.

"I sure hope so," Rowena replied, pulling off her black leather gloves. "I'm going to have to restock my woodpile soon. Winter is usually my favorite sea-son, but spring can't start soon enough for me this year."

"Same here." Phyllis shook her head and emitted a long sigh. "This weather is keeping all our custom-ers away, although Philo has been making several de-livery runs. Hardly a soul's been in the store all day."

Rowena bit back a smile, certain Phyllis and Philo

missed the local gossip their customers supplied as much as their business.

"Well, my cupboards are almost empty," Rowena told her, "so I may be here for a while. I want to stock up before the next storm hits."

"Go ahead and take your time," Phyllis said as the telephone rang beside her. "And check out those chocolate chip granola bars you like so much over in aisle six. They're on sale today."

"Thanks." Rowena grabbed a grocery cart and started down the produce aisle. She'd been serious about her empty cupboards. When she'd stepped onto the bathroom scale this morning after her shower, she'd been horrified to find she'd lost a pound since last week.

Thanks to Alan Rand.

It had been three days since she'd seen him, but just thinking about him still upset her. Maybe because he reminded her a little of Max Heller, a director on *Another Dawn* whom she'd dated for almost a year. At first, Max had been fun and charming. So concerned about her career and happiness.

But after a few months, that concern had started to turn obsessive. He'd wanted to make all her decisions for her. To direct every move she made, not only on camera but off. His advice had evolved from suggestions to commands to outright threats. When she finally broke up with him, he started sending her letters, pretending to be a deranged fan. Although she'd never had any definite proof he was the one behind them, she'd known it was him.

Max had been the main reason she'd finally left the

show. She'd been growing weary of the frantic pace of the city anyway and knew she didn't want to spend the rest of her life in New York. She didn't tell anyone where she was going and, thankfully, Max didn't attempt to track her down. No doubt he was trying to dominate another ingenue actress. Rowena swore she'd never let herself get trapped in such a controlling relationship again.

She mentally shook herself. That was all a long time ago. She didn't want to think about Max Heller anymore. Or about Alan Rand. But as she began bagging some oranges, she couldn't help but wonder if Alan was still in town. Either he'd already gone back to Toronto or he was holed up in his room at Twin Oaks.

She placed a head of lettuce into her cart, then pushed it into the next aisle. Slowing her step, she let her gaze wander over the colorful jars of baby food lined up on the shelves. Strained green beans. Strained chicken and rice. Strained peaches. She smiled, wondering which her baby would like best. There was such a wide variety to choose from. And not only in the baby food section. Her gaze moved to the rows of disposable diapers, then to the different brands of formula.

So many decisions to make. Decisions she should be enjoying during this special time, instead of worrying about what kind of bribe Alan would try next.

She pushed the cart over to a small display of stuffed animals near the end of the aisle, intrigued by a cute little purple giraffe that rattled when you shook it. Rubbing the soft fur against her cheek, she sighed, then placed it back in the display bin. She had plenty of time to buy it before the baby was born.

Besides, the last thing she wanted to do was pique Phyllis Cooper's curiosity about why she would buy such a thing now, before she'd even announced her pregnancy. Although she knew she couldn't keep her baby a secret much longer, Rowena wasn't about to make the announcement until Alan was out of the picture.

Rounding the corner, she almost bumped into another grocery cart. "Excuse me..." The words trailed off as she looked into the face of her nemesis.

"Hello, Rowena," Alan said. He looked as handsome as ever in a pine green pullover sweater and faded blue denim jeans that hugged his narrow hips and muscular legs.

So much for her hope that he'd gone back to Canada. She sucked in a deep breath. No matter what he said today, she wouldn't let him upset her. "This is a surprise. What are you doing here?"

"Just picking up a few necessities."

She looked in his cart, dismayed to find it almost half full. She saw toothpaste, bananas, oranges, tomato juice, bottled water and three boxes of chocolate chip granola bars. Enough items to bring a big smile to Phyllis Cooper's face. "Just how long are you planning to stay in Cooper's Corner?"

"Awhile," he replied vaguely, his gaze falling to her mouth for a moment, then meeting her eyes once more.

To her irritation, a blush warmed her cheeks. She

hated the effect Alan seemed to have on her. "Are you stalking me now?"

"Hey, I was in the store first."

"Why are you interfering in my life?" she asked, searching the shelf for the granola bars. When she saw it was empty, she glared at his cart. "And why are you hogging all the granola bars? Has it become your goal in life to try and take away everything I want?"

"I like granola bars," he explained calmly. "And I don't want to take your baby away from you. I just want to be a father."

"Keep your voice down," she admonished, then cast a look around. But the aisle was empty except for the two of them. She turned to him. "Why are you still here, Alan? Your home is Toronto. I won't interfere in your life in any way. All I ask is that you show me the same consideration."

A muscle flexed in his jaw. "This isn't about us," he said in a husky whisper. "It's about the baby. I can't just walk away."

"Can't or won't?" she asked. "You don't even want this baby, remember?" Just the memory of his arrogance infuriated her. "You wanted me to get rid of it!"

"That's not true." He took a step closer to her. "You made the wrong assumption the other day, Rowena. I would never ask you to terminate this pregnancy. I did some research before I came to Cooper's Corner and found one of the best obstetricians in the state. I wanted you to go to him and I intended to pay for everything. That's why I wrote out that check. To prove to you that I plan to support this baby. To help you out every step of the way.''

"We don't need your money, Alan.''

"I know the baby needs a father,'' he said, his voice rising. "And you know it, too, Rowena. I can see it in your eyes.''

So now he was telepathic. Her hands tightened on the cart handle. "Lots of children grow up without fathers and do just fine.''

"That may be true,'' he agreed. "But at the moment, all I care about is my child. And I damn well intend to be part of his life. As soon as I take that paternity test, you'll know beyond a doubt that I am the father and—''

"I already know it,'' she interjected.

He blinked. "What?''

"You don't need to take a paternity test,'' she said tightly. "The Orr Clinic confirmed that your sperm deposit was used to impregnate me.''

He nodded, relief flashing in his eyes. "So now we can start making plans for the future.''

The pounding of her heart made it difficult to think. He was so tall. So…male. "Not so fast, Alan. I think you should know I've already consulted with my attorney.''

"So have I,'' he countered. "And your lawyer probably told you the same thing. That this will be a big mess to work out in the courts, if it gets that far, but that I definitely have a case.''

So much for her hope he would back down gracefully. "Is this really how you want to start the baby's life? With a battle between its parents?''

"No." He folded his arms across his broad chest. "I'd prefer it if you'd simply recognize my rights as this baby's father."

"It's not as simple as you want to believe," she replied. "I refuse to have my child shuttled back and forth between two countries for the next eighteen years."

His eyes darkened. "And I refuse to allow *my* child to grow up believing his father doesn't care. I'm the father of your baby, Rowena. The fact that you're not happy about it doesn't change anything. I think it's time for you to accept the inevitable."

Rowena could see he was as implacable as he'd been the last time she'd seen him. It was like talking to a brick wall. This conversation wasn't getting them anywhere. "And I think you should stop telling me what to do."

Abruptly she turned away from him and grabbed the last box of detergent off the middle shelf. A weathered face peered out from the opening on the other side.

"Philo," she cried, jumping back in surprise. "What are you doing?"

"Dusting," he replied, holding up a feather duster in his hand to prove it. Then he cast his curious gaze toward Alan. "Hope I'm not interrupting anything."

Rowena swallowed a groan. She had no doubt Philo had heard every word of their conversation. "No, not at all."

"Good." Philo swiped the feather duster over the immaculate shelf. "I'll just leave you two alone now.'' Then he was gone. Probably in a hurry to fill his wife in on this latest morsel of local gossip.

She whirled on Alan. ''Now look what you've done!''

''Me?'' he replied, having the audacity to look innocent. ''All I did was come in here for a tube of toothpaste and some snacks. You're the one who brought up the subject of the baby.''

''Now everyone in Cooper's Corner will know I'm pregnant,'' she cried, too upset to care who was at fault. ''Even worse, they'll think you're the father.''

His jaw tightened. ''I *am* the father.''

Grabbing her cart, she barreled down the aisle. ''Leave me alone, Alan. From now on, if you want to talk to me, do it through my lawyer.''

She abandoned the cart at the door and walked out of the store with Phyllis staring after her. Standing on the curb, she wrapped her coat more tightly around her, knowing she shouldn't let Alan affect her this way, much less chase her out of the store. She needed to eat, no matter how much trouble he caused in her life. Cooper's Corner was too small for her to avoid him.

And why should she try? This was her town. Her home. Alan Rand was the interloper. Her nightmare with Max had taught her that the very worst thing she could do was back down from him—either in the grocery store or in a courtroom.

The winter air cooled her temper as she stood on the sidewalk. She didn't need to panic. The baby wouldn't be born until July. He'd never stick around Cooper's Corner for that long. Alan had a life in Toronto. A high-powered job in publishing. Once he realized she couldn't be browbeaten or bullied, he'd leave her alone.

She turned to walk inside and resume her shopping when the door opened and Alan stepped out.

"Are you always this high-strung?" he asked, two bulging grocery bags in his arms.

"Are you always this much of a control freak?"

"I'm just staking my claim, Rowena. The baby belongs to both of us."

She clenched her teeth, wondering why it was so easy for him to goad her. Then she forced a smile, using every ounce of her acting talent to portray a calmness she was far from feeling. "Here in America, possession is nine-tenths of the law. And right now, this baby belongs to me."

"Don't fight me on this, Rowena." His gaze narrowed on her. "I will do whatever is necessary to win this case."

"So will I," she vowed.

A wry smile tipped up the corner of his mouth. "With two parents as determined as we are, our baby will probably grow up to become prime minister."

"I think you mean president," she countered, brushing past him as she walked into the store. For once, she'd gotten in the last word.

He'd better get used to it.

THIRTY MINUTES later, Rowena pulled her car up to the post office, the back seat full of groceries. Cooper's Corner no longer had a mailman, so the residents picked up their mail each day from a post office box.

She met Keegan Cooper at the door, his arms full of envelopes and packages for Twin Oaks.

"Hey, there," she said, bending to pick up a magazine he'd dropped. "Do you need a lift home? It's quite a walk all the way to Twin Oaks."

"Nah, my dad's coming to pick me up in a few minutes. He's just over at the library checking out some videotapes for one of our guests." Keegan grinned. "Tapes about you."

A prickle of apprehension skittered up her spine. "About me?"

He nodded. "Yeah, those old *Another Dawn* videotapes. I think Mr. Rand is a big fan. He's been asking all sorts of questions about you."

Despite the cold, Rowena's anger at the man flared hot once again.

"Is something wrong?" Keegan asked, tilting his head toward her. "You look kinda mad."

"No," she replied, forcing her anger aside. Alan Rand could watch those tapes until his eyeballs fell out. He'd never find anything to use against her in court, if that was his intention. "I'm fine." She gave the boy a reassuring smile. "How about you? Is school going well?"

He shrugged. "I guess. The only thing the girls want to talk about is the Sweetheart Dance."

"Do you have a date yet?"

He grimaced. "No. I don't want one, either."

"Are you sure?" she teased. "I'm still available. Or you could ask Alison." She pointed toward the post office. Alison Fairchild was the local postmistress and had lived in Cooper's Corner all of her twenty-eight years. "You could show up with one of us and make all those girls at school jealous."

A flush stole up his cheeks. "Don't you think you're both a little too old for me?"

"You're probably right." She bit back a smile, not wanting to embarrass him anymore. He was such a sweet kid who tried to act so grown up. "But save me a dance anyway, okay?"

"I guess." Keegan moved closer to her on the sidewalk. "So Alison doesn't have a date to the dance?"

"I don't think so. Why?"

He shrugged his thin shoulders. "I don't know. I mean, she seems like a nice lady and she's not married yet or anything."

Rowena grinned. "I thought you just said she was too old for you."

Keegan rolled his eyes. "She is. But she's not too old for my dad, and he doesn't have a date for the Sweetheart Dance, either."

"Oh," Rowena said softly, her heart touched by the little matchmaker. She'd heard that Keegan's mother had passed away shortly before Clint and his son moved to Cooper's Corner. Now it seemed Keegan was trying to fill the void in their lives.

She thought of her own situation. Would her child try to play matchmaker for Rowena, as well? If she succeeded in keeping Alan out of their lives, would her child feel a void there, too?

The thought was sobering and not one she wanted to consider at the moment. She reached out to pull Keegan's knit hat over one protruding red ear. "I think your dad might prefer to pick out his own date."

Keegan looked skeptical as he shifted the mail in his arms. "Maybe you're right. Alison is real nice and all, but... Well, you know."

Keegan didn't have to spell it out for her. Unfortunately, it was as plain as the nose on Alison's face. The very large nose.

"Looks aren't everything, you know," Rowena told him. "It's what's on the inside that counts."

He rolled his eyes again. "Yeah, right."

The honk of a car horn forestalled her reply.

"There's my dad," Keegan said, moving toward the street. "See you later, Rowena."

"Bye, Keegan." She waved to Clint, then walked up the steps leading to the post office.

Alison wasn't at the counter, so Rowena walked over to the rows of post office boxes. She retrieved a handful of envelopes from the one belonging to her, as well as the latest *Hair Today* magazine.

"Good afternoon, Rowena," Alison said, leaning over the marble counter. "Can you fit me in for a haircut tonight?"

"Sure, what time?" Rowena said, moving in her direction. After her conversation with Keegan, she couldn't keep her gaze from straying to the younger woman's nose. It *was* unusually large. So large it distracted from her pretty blond hair and blue eyes. Alison was always trying a new hairstyle to minimize her most prominent feature.

"How about six o'clock?" Alison said. "Right after I get off work."

"Sounds good. I'll see you then." Rowena turned toward the door. As she walked out of the post office, her gaze fell to the mail in her hands, and she began flipping through the letters. Mostly bills and junk mail.

But it was the eerily familiar powder blue envelope that made her blood run cold.

CHAPTER SEVEN

ALAN CHEWED on a chocolate chip granola bar as he drove his car past Twin Oaks and then headed north on Highway 7. He needed time to think. Time to wonder if Rowena might be right.

Could his presence in his child's life really be detrimental? His gut instinct was to deny such a ridiculous notion, but he'd been the editor of too many books on child psychology not to consider the possible consequences.

What if he was projecting his lousy childhood onto this baby? George Rand had been physically present in Alan's life but never acted as if he cared about his only son. It still perplexed Alan, even after all these years. Had Alan done something wrong? Had their personalities clashed? Or had George never wanted to become a father?

These were questions only one man could answer.

Two hours later, Alan found himself in Albany, parked along the curb outside his father's house. George Rand might not have visited him while he was undergoing cancer treatments, but he had sent a get-well card with his return address on the envelope.

Alan stared at the small brick ranch house. Neatly trimmed bushes lined the front. Christmas lights still hung from the eaves. A black oil mark stained the empty driveway. It was the home of his father. A home he'd never known.

Should he go up and knock on the door? Ask his father the questions that had plagued him as long as he could remember?

Why didn't I matter to you? Why didn't you want to be a father? Why don't you love me?

The car idled for twenty minutes while Alan tried to decide if he really wanted to know the answers. At last, he pulled out a Twin Oaks Bed and Breakfast business card he'd picked up when he'd checked in. Then he scribbled a simple message on the back, telling his father he'd be at Twin Oaks for the next couple of weeks.

The rest was up to George.

Alan got out of the car and walked up to the house. Instead of knocking, he slipped the card into the screen door. As he drove back to Cooper's Corner, the situation with Rowena and the baby, which had been so cloudy before, now seemed perfectly clear.

He never wanted his child sitting outside a strange house, wondering if he was welcome inside. Alan knew down into his soul that he could be a good father. A loving father. A father who cared.

Now he just needed the chance to prove it.

THE NEXT DAY, Rowena stood in her shop behind the barber's chair, carefully combing out Maureen's long hair before she trimmed the ends. The afternoon sun shone through the windows, belying the bitter cold temperature outside. "Would you like to try some of the new shampoo that just came in?"

Maureen hesitated, then said gently, "That's the third time you've asked me that question in the last ten minutes, Rowena. I don't mean to pry, but is something wrong?"

So much for her intention never to bring her personal problems to work. Rowena wanted her shop to be a place her customers could relax and unwind. A place that brought them comfort. She was used to counseling people who sat in her chair. It came with the job. But her fingers shook as she ran the comb through Maureen's hair, and she knew she had to talk to someone.

"I'm sorry," she said, placing the comb on the tray next to her. "I guess I am a little preoccupied today. Maybe more than a little."

Maureen twisted around in the chair. "Is it because you know Alan Rand is the father of your baby?"

Rowena froze. "How did you know…" she began, then groaned as realization dawned. "Philo told you about it, didn't he? I was trying to convince myself he wasn't eavesdropping in the general store, but I should have known better. Please tell me the news isn't all over town already."

Maureen nodded. "I'm afraid it is. I've heard it from at least three people."

Rowena came around the chair to face her. "What exactly did you hear?"

"That you're pregnant and the father is a guest at Twin Oaks. Since Alan is the only single man staying there, it wasn't hard to figure out his identity."

Rowena sank into one of the drier chairs and buried her face in her hands. "This is a nightmare. First Alan, and now…" She couldn't put her new problem into words. "Why is this happening to me?"

Maureen was instantly at her side, a comforting arm around her shoulders. "Are you okay?"

Sucking in a deep breath, Rowena slowly lifted her head. "I will be. I *have* to be." She gave a mirthless laugh. "The last thing this baby needs is a crazy mother."

Maureen gave her shoulders a reassuring squeeze. "I think you deserve to go a little crazy once in a while, considering the circumstances."

If only the circumstances didn't keep changing. She'd been fully prepared to bring a baby into this world alone—until Alan Rand showed up to make his demands. Her perfect life was starting to crumble around the edges, and Rowena didn't know what to do about it.

She turned to Maureen. "So now that you know about him, tell me your impression of Alan."

Maureen considered the question. "I've only really seen him a couple of times at breakfast. At least now I know why he expressed such an interest in you. He didn't strike me as the kind of man who watched soap operas."

"Do you like him?"

Maureen shrugged. "He seems nice enough. Friendly. Courteous."

Her throat grew tight. "Unless you have something he wants."

"What do you mean?"

She looked at Maureen in surprise. "Didn't Philo tell everyone about the big blowup Alan and I had at the general store?"

"He might have mentioned something about a lovers' spat."

Rowena groaned. "I don't know which is worse. Having everyone in town know that I'm pregnant or having them think Alan and I are lovers. Why couldn't Philo keep his big mouth shut?"

Maureen gently brushed Rowena's hair off her face. "Philo and Phyllis don't mean any real harm. They truly do care about the people here."

"I know," Rowena admitted. "It's just that I wanted to have the chance to announce my pregnancy in my own time. My own way."

"I'm afraid Philo and Phyllis beat you to it." Maureen smiled. "But the news isn't all bad. Last I heard, Phyllis was organizing a baby shower for you."

Rowena tried to smile, but her lips trembled. Would her roller-coaster emotions ever come under control? "She'd better include an invitation for Alan Rand, or he'll probably take her to court, too."

Maureen's eyes widened. "He's taking you to court?"

Rowena nodded. "He wants to assert his rights as the father of the baby."

"Sounds complicated."

"It is. Alan is demanding to be a part of my baby's life. He's made it abundantly clear that he won't stop until he obtains his rights as father. That includes generous visitation, possibly even joint custody."

"And you're opposed?"

"Of course I'm opposed!" She hated the tremble she heard in her voice. "Alan Rand is a controlling pain in the butt. I have enough to deal with in my life right now without him causing more trouble."

Maureen pursed her lips, her green eyes too discerning. "Rowena, what's really wrong? There's something else, isn't there?"

Rowena stood up and walked behind the counter. The front shelves were filled with rows of shampoo, conditioner and assorted styling gels in a variety of colors. Reaching into a wire mesh basket on the top shelf, she retrieved the powder blue envelope. "This came in the mail yesterday."

Pulling her arms from under the vinyl cape she wore, Maureen reached for the envelope. "It's addressed to Savannah Corrington. That was the name of your character on *Another Dawn*."

Rowena nodded. "It's common for viewers to know actors by their role rather than their real name."

"So is it from one of your fans?"

"Just the opposite, I'm afraid." Rowena leaned wearily against the counter. She'd been unable to sleep well after reading the letter, and her entire body ached with exhaustion. But at least the awful tension that had been building inside her had dissipated.

Once she'd unfolded the letter from the envelope, Maureen began to read it aloud.

"'My darling Savannah, I love you so very much. How could you leave me? Don't you know our love is endless. We were so very special together. I never should have let you go. Do you dream of me as I dream of you? Soon, I hope those dreams will become reality. My love is forever. Your devoted Sloane.'''

Maureen's gaze skimmed over the letter a second time. "Who is Sloane?"

"He was my love interest on the show. But the letter isn't from the actor who played him."

"Then who is it from?"

"Max Heller. An ex-boyfriend."

"You're sure."

Rowena sighed. "Almost positive, although I don't have any proof."

"So why do you think he's responsible?"

"Because I started getting those same kind of letters right after I broke up with him. On the same powder blue stationery. I think he wanted to scare me back into his arms by making me believe a deranged stalker was after me. I finally confronted him about the letters, and he denied it, but I never got another one after that."

Maureen flipped over the envelope. "There's no return address, although the postmark shows it came from New York. When did the letters start up again?"

"That's what's so odd," Rowena replied. "This is the first one since I moved to Cooper's Corner six years ago. I guess I wrongly assumed that meant Max didn't know where to find me."

"Maybe the resurrection of Savannah Corrington on *Another Dawn* set him off again."

"That's what I thought." Rowena pulled up the stool behind her and sat down. Her shoes pinched, and she knew before long her feet would start to swell— along with her stomach. Now that the entire town knew of her pregnancy, she could start shopping for maternity clothes. "Did I ever tell you the executive producers of *Another Dawn* approached me last summer and offered me the role again? Along with a generous signing bonus."

Maureen tucked the letter into the envelope. "No, but I wondered. I take it you turned them down?"

She nodded. "I like my life here. At least, I did before Alan Rand came to town. I guess it could be worse, though," she said, suppressing a shiver. "At least Max hasn't shown up yet."

"He sounds mentally unstable."

Rowena shook her head. "Max might go to extremes, but I don't think he's actually crazy. Just very controlling. He wants to direct the people in life like he directs the actors on a set."

"What if the letters never were from Max? What if it was just a coincidence that you stopped receiving them after your confrontation with him?"

"I suppose that's a possibility." Then she shook her head. "No, it sounds too much like him to be anyone else. Declaring his undying love at the same time he's trying to make me feel guilty."

Maureen set the letter on the counter. "I think you should contact the police. Just to be safe."

"They won't be able to do anything. Not on the basis of one letter and not unless Max makes some kind of overt physical threat. I've been through this before." Rowena thought back to those years she'd lived in New York. How isolated she'd felt in a city with over seven million people. Strange how it all seemed like a lifetime ago.

Maureen scowled. "Did this Max ever try to hurt you?"

She hesitated. "One day after shooting on the set, he wanted to take me out to lunch. This was after I'd broken up with him and I knew he wanted to try to resurrect the relationship. When I refused to go, he tracked me down in the parking lot, grabbed my arm and started pulling me toward his car. I was dragged several feet before the security guards finally intervened."

"That's horrible," Maureen exclaimed. "Please tell me he was arrested."

"I filed a police report, but the producers of the show convinced me not to press charges. They promised to make Max stay away from me, and surprisingly, he did."

"But you still left the show."

"Max was just one of the reasons. Did I ever tell you how I got the role of Savannah in the first place?"

Maureen smiled. "No, but I'd love to hear it."

"I never planned to be an actress. I wanted to be a hairdresser like my mother. Making people feel good about themselves is the best feeling in the world. So I went to cosmetology school, then got lucky enough to land an internship on *Another Dawn* to assist the stylists there. I learned some fabulous tricks of the trade."

"Like helping my two little girls look good again after they decided to play hairstylist with each other."

Rowena laughed. "Yes. I love my work. I did back then, too. But one day a director rushed in and grabbed me for a walk-on role."

"A role that grew into one of the most popular characters on daytime television."

Rowena nodded. "Max was the director who *discovered* me. Maybe that's one of the reasons I stayed with him as long as I did. But eventually, I found myself spending more and more time in the hair and makeup station. After the last confrontation with Max, I decided I just wasn't happy anymore. So I told the show I wanted to leave, and that's how I ended up here."

"Do you ever miss acting?"

Rowena smiled. "The acting bug never bit me that hard. I'm perfectly content taking part in the Christmas play every year."

"We're lucky to have you," Maureen said, then her smile faded. "But I'm still concerned about this letter. I think you should at least notify the police in New York and ask them to keep an eye on him."

"I will if they keep coming," she promised. "Max must be between girlfriends. Maybe if I just ignore the letter, he'll leave me alone again. I really don't believe he's dangerous."

Maureen looked doubtful. "I'm not sure you should take the chance. Sometimes waiting for the unknown can be more frightening than confronting it."

"I know you're probably right." Rowena waved Maureen over to the barber's chair, then picked up her comb and scissors. "But for now I'd rather confront my more immediate problem."

Maureen sat down, draping the vinyl cape over her clothes. "You mean Alan Rand?"

"He's incredibly stubborn," Rowena said as she began clipping the ends of Maureen's long hair.

"Handsome, too."

"I noticed," Rowena said wryly.

"So what's your next move?"

"I wish I knew."

Maureen didn't say anything for several minutes, the steady clip of the scissors the only sound filling the air.

"Why not try to make Alan your ally instead of your enemy?" Maureen suggested. "You're a beautiful, intelligent woman, Rowena. Few men can resist that combination. Perhaps now is the right time to use it to your advantage."

Rowena laughed, realizing it was the first time she'd done so in several days. "I think you overestimate my powers of persuasion."

"What can it hurt?" Maureen ventured. "The way I see it, you have nothing to lose and everything to gain."

"I hate to admit it, but that does make sense." She brushed some stray clippings off the back of Maureen's neck. "Do you have any idea when Alan plans to check out of Twin Oaks?"

"I'm afraid not. He made an open-ended reservation."

"If he can afford such a long vacation, money must not be a factor for him. So I guess I won't be able to bribe Mr. Rand out of my life."

Maureen smiled. "Now tell the truth. Would you really try to do that?"

Rowena laughed again. "Only if my plot to kidnap

him and dump him on a deserted island fails. An island with lots of hungry ants.''

"There's nothing like a little revenge fantasy to make a girl feel better.''

"My thoughts exactly.'' She pulled the nylon cape off Maureen and brushed a few stray hairs from her collar. "There you go. No charge today. In fact, I should be the one paying you for letting me cry on your shoulder.''

"Forget it,'' Maureen replied, pulling her checkbook out of her purse. "The shoulder is free. So is the advice. I've noticed Alan likes honey for breakfast. You might consider using some on him.''

CHAPTER EIGHT

THE NEXT DAY, Maureen couldn't get her mind off that strange letter Rowena had received. Was it really from a disgruntled ex-boyfriend? A man who sounded as if he could turn violent if provoked. Or worse, one of those delusional people who thought the characters on a soap opera were real. Had one of Rowena's fans taken offense when a new actress reprised the role?

Maureen pondered these unsettling questions as she swept the kitchen floor, played with the twins and made pleasant small talk during the afternoon tea. But she grew more and more uneasy as the day went on. She'd lived with her fear of Owen Nevil for over a year now. It had affected her daily life—even the way she viewed strangers.

Last fall an anonymous letter had been sent to Maureen at the New York Police Department. A letter marked personal. The cryptic message still sent a chill down her spine. *You can't hide from me. I will find you.*

Knowing that Rowena had to endure that same kind of psychological fear made her want to do something about it. Maybe Rowena's letter was from a relatively harmless ex-boyfriend with too much time on his hands. Or a disgruntled fan.

But maybe it was something more.

As a former police officer, she was well aware of the danger a stalker could pose. A danger not only to Rowena, but to the baby she carried inside her. While Maureen understood Rowena's reluctance to involve the police, she didn't agree with it.

Still, there might be a way she could help her friend without causing more disruption in her life. Since moving to Cooper's Corner, Maureen seldom had contact with her old colleagues from the New York Police Department. The fewer connections she kept with her old life, the less chance one of them could inadvertently lead Nevil to her. But she did maintain frequent contact with Frank Quigg, the captain of the NYPD detective unit.

A simple phone call to Frank about Rowena's letter would give her peace of mind. He could check into it, see if Max Heller was up to his old tricks or if the threat was coming from another source. She nodded as she cleared the last of the teacups off the dining room table, her mind made up. She'd call Frank right away.

Maureen checked on Randi and Robin, who were playing with dolls in their room, then made her way to the office to place the call.

Her old captain answered on the first ring. "Quigg here."

"Hi, Frank. It's Maureen."

"Hello, stranger. Good to hear from you." His gravelly voice was set against a backdrop of ringing telephones and general commotion. For one fleeting moment, the chaotic sounds made her miss her old job.

"Is this a bad time?" she asked, after the wave of nostalgia had passed. Her old life was behind her. Cooper's Corner was the best place for Maureen. The perfect place to raise her girls.

"Not at all. I was just about to take my afternoon coffee break."

She smiled. Frank hadn't taken a break for the last thirty years. The department kept him too busy. He was a seasoned pro who went strictly by the book. She trusted him with her life.

"So what's up?" Frank asked, never one to mince words. "Any sign of Owen Nevil?"

"No," she replied. "Nothing out of the ordinary. We're busier than ever around here. Full up the entire month of February."

"No suspicious guests?"

His question didn't surprise her. About a month after the letter with that cryptic message arrived at her old office, she and Clint discovered a guest had registered using a phony name and occupation. Quigg learned the man was a private investigator from New York. Hired by Owen Nevil? She still didn't know the answer to that question.

"I've verified everyone," she replied. "In fact, I'm calling for a favor."

"Name it," he said without a moment's hesitation.

"I have a friend who might be in danger...."

ALAN STARED at the television set, his potato chip poised in midair.

"Don't leave me, Savannah. You're the only good thing in my life. The only thing that matters."

"I'm sorry, Sloane. I have to go back to Derrick. He needs me."

Alan brought the chip slowly to his mouth, his eyes never leaving the screen.

"What about us, Savannah?" Sloane pulled her into his arms. "Can you really leave me? Leave... this?" He bent his head to kiss her.

Alan picked up the remote control and hit the fast-forward button. After watching four episodes of *Another Dawn,* he'd developed a deep hatred for Sloane. But he couldn't seem to take his eyes off Rowena. She was incredible in the role of spitfire Savannah Corrington. Poised, clever and coolly manipulative.

What mesmerized him most were the glimpses he saw of the real Rowena. Her contagious smile. That tiny wrinkle in her brow when she was perplexed. The flash of fire in her beautiful amethyst eyes. Fire sparked by anger—or passion.

There was only one part of the show he didn't enjoy—Savannah's hot affair with the lead male character. Who could miss the proprietary way Sloane held Rowena when he kissed her? Or those uncomfortable scenes where they shared a bed, their naked shoulders above the silk sheets giving the illusion of complete nudity. Alan knew it was all staged, but he'd reached a point where he had to fast-forward through all the love scenes or go crazy.

Crazy seemed to be the best word to describe him whenever he was around Rowena. Like their confrontation in the general store. He handled sensitive negotiations with tempestuous writers in his business all the time. So why should his dealings with Rowena be any different?

There was something about the woman that made him lose all rational thought. Something about the shape of her full pink mouth that made him crave kissing her. A craving he'd tried unsuccessfully to satisfy with the greasy potato chips he'd bought on impulse this afternoon. Alan stared in distaste at the empty bag on the bed beside him.

As the credits rolled at the end of another episode, Alan hit the stop button on the remote control. It had been a long day. Ed had given him an expansive tour of the village of Cooper's Corner and the surrounding area. Alan had met several people happy to discuss the gorgeous barber, and what they had to say didn't surprise him.

Everyone loved Rowena Dahl. From the postmistress to the librarian to the Episcopalian minister. They used words like *sweet, kind* and *thoughtful* to describe her, which didn't exactly fit the hellcat she played with him. Her claws came out whenever he tried to assert his rights to his baby.

Alan sighed, then reluctantly reached for his briefcase. He knew it was past time to get started on the work he'd brought with him. He couldn't generate any enthusiasm for it—a problem that had plagued him for the last several months. He looked over the list of standard contract clauses his company reassessed every few years. Normally, he'd go over them with a fine-tooth comb, but now he quickly scanned them, making a few minor changes, then calling it good.

Once he faxed his response to the office, he could give Rowena his full concentration.

Grabbing the file, he left the room and bounded down the stairs. A young couple snuggled together on the love seat near the hearth, oblivious to his presence. He could hear the sound of pans clanging in the kitchen as he walked toward the office shared by Clint and Maureen Cooper. The door was closed but not latched. As he pushed it open, his footsteps muted by a thick carpet, he heard Maureen's voice.

"Yes, Frank, her name is Rowena Dahl. That's spelled D-A-H-L. And I really do believe she may be in some danger. I was hoping you could assign one of your officers to look into the matter."

Alan stepped back, pulling the door with him. But he left it cracked open far enough to hear the telephone conversation.

At first, Alan thought Maureen was referring to him as the danger in Rowena's life. But why would she be contacting a cop? He hadn't done anything illegal.

"Yes, the letter arrived today," Maureen continued. Alan knew she was unaware of his presence outside the door. "Powder blue stationery with a postmark from New York, but no return address on the envelope. The letter itself was signed with the name Sloane, but I don't think that will help us at all. Sloane was Rowena's love interest on the soap opera *Another Dawn*."

Alan's ethical standards were falling fast. First pumping the townspeople for information about Rowena and now eavesdropping. But if Rowena was in danger, so was his baby. He needed to know for sure. Damn it, he had a *right* to know.

"Not Rowena's love interest," Maureen clarified. "Her character's love interest." Another pause. "Yes, I know it's confusing. But Rowena believes the man who sent the letter is a man named Max Heller. He was a director on the show when she worked there."

Alan hated hearing a one-sided conversation. Why would Rowena be in danger from a director? The cop on the other end must have asked the same question.

"Yes, they were involved several years ago. Apparently, Heller is a control freak who wasn't happy when she broke up with him."

Alan waited, the long silence making him grow even more tense. *Control freak.* Hadn't Rowena accused him of the same thing?

"No, there wasn't an outright threat in the letter," Maureen said. "But it was definitely implied. This isn't the first time she's received this type of letter. But since she has no real evidence it's from Heller, we don't know for sure if he's the one responsible or someone else. Although Heller assaulted her in a parking lot once several years ago."

Something cold wrapped itself around Alan's gut and wouldn't let go. *Assaulted?*

"Thank you, Frank," Maureen said, "I really appreciate your help." A long pause. "Yes, I'm sure everything is fine. I'll definitely keep my eyes open. Be sure and let me know if you hear anything on your end."

Sensing the phone conversation was coming to a

close, Alan slowly backed away from the door. He didn't want to believe what he'd just heard.

"Alan?"

He spun around, surprised to see Rowena standing in front of him. Her butter blond hair floated around her shoulders. She looked so beautiful. So… vulnerable.

He swallowed hard, resisting the urge to sweep her into his arms and keep her safe. "Hello."

She shifted from one foot to the other. "I was wondering if we could talk."

"Sure. Go ahead."

She looked around the room, her gaze falling on the couple cuddling by the fire. "I'd rather go somewhere private, if you don't mind. What I have to say may surprise you."

ROWENA FOLLOWED ALAN into his room on the upper floor of Twin Oaks. She looked around, realizing she'd never been in one of the cozy guest rooms before. The decor was charming and quaint. The overall effect, especially with a fire blazing in the hearth, was definitely romantic.

"Please sit down," Alan said, holding out a chair.

She walked over to him, realizing that for all his threats to take her to court, he wasn't nearly as frightening as the man who had sent her that creepy fan letter.

Alan sat on the bed across from her and waited for her to speak first.

It wasn't going to be easy. But Alan Rand was the father of her baby and he wasn't going away. It was time for her to deal with that fact. And if possible, find a way to make the best of it.

"I want to call a truce," she began. "Maybe we can start over. Get to know each other better before we decide what's best for the baby."

He arched a brow. "A truce?"

She gave a jerky nod. "I know it will be... complicated."

Surely she could find some way to convince him that the worst thing for their baby would be shuttling it back and forth between two countries. If nothing else, she could make him aware of how much care a child needed. The heavy responsibilities. How completely Alan's life would change.

"Believe it or not, I don't want to cause complications for you or the baby," Alan said. "No matter how it might seem to you, I think having two parents is a good thing."

"Except one of us will be in Canada," she said with a sigh. "And one in Massachusetts."

"I believe we can find a way to make it work."

She licked her dry lips, trying not to notice how his gaze dropped to her mouth. "So you agree that we can start over?"

"Absolutely. And the first thing I want to do is apologize." He took a deep breath. "I'm sorry I dropped into your life without any warning. It wasn't fair to you, and I don't blame you for being upset."

She'd only met Alan Rand a few days ago, but she sensed how difficult it was for him to say that. He didn't strike her as a man who apologized often.

"I think we've both said things we regret." She

drew up her shoulders. "I'm sure neither one of us wanted to bring a baby into the world this way. But thanks to the clinic's mistake, our lives will never be the same."

"But forever entwined," he replied softly.

He might be right. If he insisted on being part of the baby's life, they'd probably celebrate all the momentous events together. Birthdays. Graduations. Maybe someday a wedding. Even the birth of grandchildren. He'd talked about fairness before. Was it fair for her to try to leave him completely out in the cold?

She mentally shook herself, wondering why she was worried about this man who had invaded her life and demanded to become a part of it. He seemed perfectly capable of taking care of himself.

But was he capable of taking care of a baby? Was he really ready to be a father? It was time for her to find out. "I'd like to invite you to dinner at my house tomorrow night. It will be a chance for us to get to know each other better."

"I accept," he said, one corner of his mouth kicking up in a smile.

Her heart flip-flopped in her chest. How could she spend time with this man and not reveal her attraction to him? What if he used it against her?

She had no choice. The baby was all that mattered.

"What time?" he asked.

She rose to her feet, disconcerted by the nervous fluttering in her stomach. A fluttering she couldn't attribute to the baby. "Around seven."

He reached the door before she did and held it open

for her. But as she started to leave, he touched her arm to detain her. "Rowena?"

She looked at his hand, lightly curled around her elbow, then into his face. It struck her that he could have been a star. He had the same natural charisma as any actor she'd ever worked with on television. The same overpowering presence. "Yes?"

His hand slid off her arm, the touch of his fingers sending delicious shivers through her. "Thank you for coming here tonight. I promise you won't regret it."

She gazed into his warm, toffee brown eyes, and warning bells rang in her head. Alan Rand had morphed into Mr. Charming again.

Which meant he was more dangerous than ever.

CHAPTER NINE

THE NEXT EVENING, the knock on her front door made Rowena's heart skip a beat. This was it—the beginning of their truce. Ever since she'd proposed it to Alan, she'd been wondering if it was the right decision.

She was about to find out.

Smoothing the recalcitrant curls in her hair, she walked quickly to the door and opened it. Alan stood on the other side in a black trench coat, holding a bottle of wine in his hands.

They stood staring at each other for a long, uncomfortable moment, then began to speak at the same time.

"Hello—"

"Good even—" Alan's voice trailed off.

"Please come in," she said, hoping the rest of the evening wouldn't be as awkward as this beginning.

He limped through the front door, then moved to the braided rug to wipe the snow off his shoes. That's when she noticed the snow clinging to one leg of his slacks all the way to the knee.

"Did you fall?"

"It's nothing," he said, wiping the snow off his

pant leg with one hand. "I just slipped on an icy patch on the sidewalk."

"On my sidewalk?" she asked, moving to look out the window. "I just salted it again this afternoon."

"I'm fine, really," he assured her. "Don't worry about it."

She closed the front door, hoping this wasn't a portent of the evening to come. When she turned, she saw his gaze taking in her small living room. The burgundy leather sofa and chair that she'd splurged on last winter. The thick, handwoven rug that lay on the polished hardwood floor in front of the crackling fire. Scented candles of varying heights flickering on the mantel.

Rowena had an eclectic decorating style. She chose items that caught her fancy rather than conformed to a certain period. Her house was small but cozy. She'd fallen in love with it the moment she saw it. She wondered what Alan thought of her home. And why she cared.

"Let me hang up your coat," she said, taking the bottle of wine out of his hands and setting it on an end table.

"The windchill must be below zero tonight," he said, unbuttoning his trench coat.

"At least there's no snow predicted for a couple of days." She hung his coat on the hall tree, then waved him into the living room.

"I used to love snow days when I was a kid." Alan sat in the chair. "It meant snowball fights and time off school. Now it means driving to work on slippery streets and scraping ice off the car windows in subzero temperatures.''

She nodded, not sure what they would talk about when they exhausted the subject of the weather. Did Alan feel as uncomfortable as she did? If so, he wasn't showing it. He settled into the chair, looking perfectly relaxed in his blue cable knit sweater and khaki slacks. A slight shadow of whiskers darkened his square jaw, and she could see the firelight reflected in his eyes.

''You look nice,'' he said abruptly.

She blinked, realizing she'd been thinking the same thing about him. For some disconcerting reason, this evening felt more like a date than a truce.

''Thank you,'' she stammered, her gaze falling to the amethyst sweater she wore, along with a pair of matching stretch pants. She'd chosen the outfit with deliberate care to look casual. So deliberate, in fact, that she'd changed clothes five times before his arrival.

Another awkward silence settled between them. Strange how they could find plenty to say when they were arguing about the baby. She knew the subject had to come up eventually.

She picked up a candy dish and held it toward him. ''Chocolate?''

''Thanks,'' he said, popping one into his mouth.

She took one, too, chewing as slowly as possible. In her line of work, Rowena was used to filling silences with easy chatter. But tonight, something about Alan made her tongue-tied. Her gaze strayed to the grandfather clock in the corner. Only ten minutes had gone by. Dinner wouldn't be ready for at least another twenty. What could they possibly talk about until then?

Alan stood up and walked to the end table. "How about if I open the wine?"

"Good idea," she said, moving to the armoire and taking out a corkscrew and a wineglass. She handed the corkscrew to him, then watched him deftly remove the cork from the bottle.

"Let me pour," she said, taking the bottle from him. She filled the wineglass with the sparkling white wine, then handed it to him.

He frowned as she placed the cork in the bottle. "Aren't you having any?"

She placed her hand lightly over her abdomen. "Alcohol is off-limits for the next few months. It's not good for the baby."

A mottled flush suffused his cheeks. "I never even thought...."

"Please don't worry about it," she assured him, oddly touched by his discomfiture. She'd seen Alan blustering, bullheaded and bossy, but never embarrassed.

He set his wineglass on the table. "If you're not having any wine, then I won't, either."

"No, please go ahead," she said, moving toward the doorway. "Sit down and relax. I need to check on dinner."

Then she escaped into the kitchen, wondering how long she could linger before he started wondering what had happened to her.

Fifteen minutes down, an eternity to go.

But much to Rowena's surprise, the time passed

more quickly once they sat down to dinner. Her baked lasagna turned out just right, and the peach cobbler that happened to be one of Alan's favorite dishes.

After a third helping, he placed his napkin on his plate, then pushed his chair back from the table. "That was a delicious meal, Rowena. Thank you."

"You're welcome," she replied, starting to gather the empty dishes. Their dinner conversation had revolved around their favorite movies and books, including a spirited discussion of the subtext in Jane Austen's *Pride and Prejudice.* But no controversial subjects like politics, religion or the baby.

Rowena knew they'd have to talk about the baby sometime, but she dreaded another argument with him. Surprisingly, she found Alan to be a witty, charming man when he wasn't putting her on the defensive.

He rose to his feet and began carrying the dirty dishes into the kitchen.

"You don't need to do that," she said, following him with her hands full. "Especially with your sore knee."

"My knee is fine," he assured her, setting the dishes on the counter.

"I mean it, Alan, I can handle this. Besides, I was just going to clear the table." Rowena placed the lid on the dessert pan. "I'll wash dishes later."

But Alan was already filling the sink with hot, soapy water. "Let me do them. You're the one who's pregnant. You should probably sit down and rest."

She braced her hands on her hips. "I suppose if you had your way, I'd be spending the next six months in bed.'' Too late, she realized he could take her comment the wrong way.

And judging by the way his eyes darkened to a burnished brown, he had. A blush burned in her cheeks. Turning, she grabbed a dish towel and frantically searched for another topic of conversation. ''When I lived in New York City, I rarely cooked. There were too many great restaurants in my neighborhood.''

''Toronto is the same,'' he replied, turning to drop the soiled silverware into the sink. He seemed grateful for the change of subject. ''You can find anything from Thai food to Japanese to Egyptian. But after the meal we just had, I know you must have learned to cook somewhere.''

She moved beside him and leaned her back against the counter. ''My grandfather was actually a fabulous cook. I spent two weeks with him every summer when I was growing up, and he put me in charge of preparing the evening meal. But he'd help me every step of the way.''

''Sounds like he meant a lot to you,'' Alan said, rinsing the silverware and placing it in the drainer.

''He did.'' She picked up the forks and began drying them, her throat suddenly tight. ''He passed away two years ago.''

''My mom would have loved becoming a grandmother,'' he mused. ''She died five years ago.''

''I'm sorry,'' she replied softly. ''What about your dad?''

He didn't say anything for a long moment. ''He's not around much. What about your parents?''

"My mother's in Brazil, and my dad's on the west coast, so I don't see them often. They divorced when I was four. I think that's one of the reasons I enjoyed spending time with my grandpa. I promised him once that if I ever had a boy, I'd name my son after him."

"What was your grandpa's name?"

"Ulysses Herman."

She laughed at the horrified expression on his face. "Just kidding. His name was Joseph Aaron."

He grinned. "And here I was thinking Ulysses Herman Rand had kind of a nice ring to it. But I like Joseph Aaron Rand, too."

"I think you mean Joseph Aaron Dahl," she countered, setting a dry plate on the counter and reaching for another one.

He started to say something, then shook his head. "We don't have to decide on a name for months."

"You're right," she agreed, not wanting to disrupt the temporary harmony between them. For a moment, she'd been having fun—forgotten she didn't want him involved in decisions like naming her baby. Time to change the subject again.

"So tell me more about your family," she said. "Any brothers or sisters?"

"No." He added more hot water to the sink. "I'm an only child."

"Does your father live in Toronto, too?"

For a moment she thought he was going to ignore her question. He bent over the sink to scrub at a stubborn spot on a saucepan, then placed it in the dish drainer. "Not anymore. He moved to Albany shortly after my mother passed away. He was never a big part of my life.''

Was that the reason Alan was so insistent about being a father to this baby?

''I spent my summers with a friend of mine, Brad Haley. His family has a cabin at Lake Temagami.''

''That sounds nice.''

''It's the perfect place for kids,'' he said. ''Great fishing and rock climbing. Brad's father taught me how to do both.''

Rowena could hear the affection in his voice. So different from the remote, indifferent way he'd spoken about his own father. ''Sounds like the perfect summer vacation.''

''It was.'' He swirled the soapy dishrag inside a glass. ''That's the childhood I want for my son or daughter, Rowena. Or as close to it as possible.''

She wanted a perfect childhood for her baby, too, but she couldn't imagine spending the summers or any part of the year away from her child.

''I just hope I can be as good a father as Bradford Haley, Senior.'' A reminiscent smile curved his firm mouth. ''He could discipline me without even raising his voice. He had this way of looking at a kid that made you feel about two inches tall. But then he'd tell me what I did wrong and help me figure out how I should have handled the situation.''

''So how would he assess our situation?''

He shrugged his broad shoulders. ''I'm not sure. Although I can just imagine his expression when I try to explain it to him.''

''I think we should keep it a secret,'' she said, hoping he'd understand her concern. "This pregnancy occurred because of a mistake, but I don't ever want my baby to know it."

He gave a slow nod. "You're right. I never thought about that."

"So you agree?"

He turned to her. "Absolutely. It will be our secret."

She tilted her head to meet his gaze, realizing she'd never really looked at him this closely before. He had long, dark eyelashes that any woman would envy. A straight, aquiline nose, solid cheekbones and a firm mouth. His brown eyes reminded her of warm toffee, and she felt something melt inside her. Somehow she knew that her intended donor, the French Canadian, just didn't compare to Alan Rand.

A platter slipped out of Alan's fingers and landed in the soapy water with a splash. Another flush crept up his cheeks as he turned to retrieve it. "Sorry about that."

"No problem," she said with a smile as she wiped the soapsuds off the front of her sweater.

He cleared his throat, then handed her the wet platter. "Speaking of the Orr Clinic, you never mentioned why you decided to go all the way to Canada for the procedure."

She slowly wiped the dish towel over the surface of the platter. "My doctor recommended it."

Alan searched the soapy water for more dishes, but came up empty. "He must feel awful about it now."

"You have no idea," Rowena murmured, reaching across him to pull the rubber stopper out of the sink.

Her arm brushed his broad chest, but he didn't shy away from the contact. Instead, he turned toward her again, and their gazes locked, the only sound in the kitchen that of water swirling down the drain.

"Thank you for helping with the dishes," she said at last.

He took a step closer to her, his eyes never leaving her face. "You're welcome."

She drew in a breath, wondering if he was going to kiss her. She watched his hand come up and lightly cup her chin. Her mind told her to back away, but her feet stayed firmly planted on the floor.

Then his thumb gently swiped across the tip of her nose. He held his thumb up for her to see the soapsuds clinging to it. "You missed some."

A shaky smile rose to her lips, and her heart beat unnecessarily fast. "Thanks."

The kitchen clock chimed, breaking the invisible tether between them. Had he really been about to kiss her? Or was that just wishful thinking?

"It's getting late," he said, returning to the sink and wringing out the wet dishcloth. "I think I'd better go."

"I'll walk you out."

They both lingered at the front door, but there didn't seem to be anything else to say. "Well, good night, Rowena. And thank you again for dinner."

"Thank you for coming," she replied as he walked out the door. "And watch out for that slippery spot."

He waved, then headed for his car, one foot sliding on the sidewalk before he regained his balance. She waited until he drove away from the curb before she closed the front door.

Their first evening together had gone better than she'd expected. Alan could be warm and witty. The stories he'd told about his childhood and his distant father had touched her. And made her understand a little bit better why this baby was so important to him.

But how long could their truce last? For the most part, they'd steered clear of any in-depth discussion about the baby. That couldn't last forever. Even the subject of a name had caused a moment of tension between them.

She shivered, more from apprehension about the coming days than the cold. Just like that icy patch on the sidewalk, there were hidden risks in becoming too close to him.

Risks she just wasn't willing to take.

ALAN TURNED OVER in bed, tugging the quilt around his shoulders. Had he been completely nuts to agree to this truce with Rowena? After he'd overheard Maureen's telephone conversation about a potential stalker, his main goal had been to protect her. But who was going to protect her from him?

He'd almost kissed her tonight. Closing his eyes, he could envision her pink lips slightly parted, her soft breath caressing his chin. He'd been within inches of paradise. Instead, he'd refrained and landed in purgatory. How could he possibly sleep?

His knee throbbed from the spill on her sidewalk. He thought about going down to the kitchen for some ice, but he'd need to apply it to more than one part of his anatomy.

It was hopeless. He couldn't deny his physical attraction to Rowena any longer. He wanted her more than he'd ever wanted any woman. But that didn't mean he had to act on it. He liked spending time with her. Felt he was making progress with her. But he was still adjusting to the idea of becoming a father. She was the mother of his child, not a potential one-night stand.

He shifted on the bed, his body not so easily convinced.

His thoughts drifted to that letter she'd received. How dare anyone try to terrorize her. And would she ever trust him enough to tell him about it? If necessary, he'd track down this Heller himself and make the man understand that Rowena was off-limits. From every man. Including Alan himself.

But he could still dream about her. That was his last thought as he finally drifted off to sleep.

CHAPTER TEN

ROWENA COULDN'T believe her eyes when she looked out her living room window the next morning. Alan was clearing the inch of snow that had fallen during the night off her sidewalk.

She grabbed her coat, slipped into her boots and stepped onto the front porch. "What are you doing out here this early?"

"Clearing the sidewalk so you don't fall."

She smiled. "Seems like you're the one who's been hitting the pavement lately."

"A few bruises won't hurt me," he replied, scooping up another shovelful of snow. "But you're pregnant, so you need to be extra careful." He straightened and wagged a finger at her. "I don't want you out here until this ice is gone."

She folded her arms across her chest. "I don't take orders, Alan. From you or anyone."

A muscle flexed in his jaw. "Even if it's for your own good?"

"I'm perfectly capable of taking care of myself."

A humorless smile crossed his lips. "I can see that. So let me rephrase what I said before. Please try to stay off the sidewalk until I get it cleared. I'd hate for you to slip and hurt yourself or the baby."

"Okay," she agreed, a little surprised he'd acquiesced so easily. "I will."

Maybe he was different from Max, after all. Her old boyfriend had always grown livid when challenged. He'd wanted complete control. Complete domination. Unlike Alan, who simply wanted to take care of her and the baby. Rowena had to admit to herself that after so many years of living on her own, it was nice to have someone looking out for her.

She watched him attack the stubborn patch of ice with the shovel, trying unsuccessfully to break it apart. "Come on in when you want to take a break. I'll make us some hot chocolate."

Alan looked up to watch her disappear inside the house. Did the woman have any idea how damn beautiful she was without even trying? This morning she wore a light blue sweat suit and no makeup, her long blond hair pulled back into a loose ponytail. But just the sight of her and the warmth of her smile had made him impervious to the cold.

Twenty minutes later, he walked inside the house, kicking off his wet boots on the mat by the door. He shrugged out of his jacket and hung it on the hall tree. Then he blew on his stiff hands.

"Perfect timing," Rowena said, appearing from the kitchen with two steaming mugs in her hands. "I hope you like whipped cream with your hot chocolate."

"Is there any other way to drink it?" He took a mug from her, welcoming the warmth against his fingers. Hot chocolate on a cold winter's day was one of his favorite things. That list of favorites had grown recently. Now it included old episodes of *Another Dawn* and amethyst eyes.

She curled up on the sofa. "You look completely frozen."

"Close, but not quite," he replied, joining her there.

"Thank you for clearing my sidewalk."

"My pleasure," he said, then grinned. "Well, maybe pleasure isn't the right word. I can think of other things I'd rather do for you."

When he saw roses bloom in her cheeks, he realized she'd misunderstood his meaning. But Alan didn't rush to clarify himself. It made him wonder if he wasn't the only one feeling this pull between them.

"More hot chocolate?" she asked.

"No, thanks, this is fine." He hid a yawn behind his hand. "Sorry, I didn't sleep too well last night."

Rowena blew on her drink, not meeting his gaze. "You do look tired."

"It's this peaceful country life," he said with a smile. "I can usually sleep through anything in the city—sirens, barking dogs, horns honking. But it's too quiet out here. I'm exhausted."

"What about a baby?"

His brow creased. "What about it?"

"You just said you're a heavy sleeper. What will you do if the baby wakes up crying in the middle of the night? Sleep right through it?"

He looked taken aback for a moment. "I don't know. I'm sure I'd wake up eventually."

"I've been doing some reading," Rowena continued. "Some babies get their days and nights turned around. They sleep all day and stay awake all night.

That won't be too much of a problem for me, because I'm self-employed and can adjust my schedule. But it might be a problem for you.''

He arched a dark brow. ''Are you trying to scare me off?''

''I'm just illustrating the realities of becoming a single parent. Most newborns need to be fed two to three times a night.''

''So I'll set my alarm clock,'' he replied.

She shook her head, wondering how far she should push it. But he needed to know what he faced as a father. ''You can't schedule a feeding like a business meeting. The baby could cry for other reasons besides hunger. Like colic. A wet diaper. An earache. Any one of a hundred things.''

''I'm sure I'll manage,'' he said with a stubborn set to his jaw.

''I hope so,'' she said softly. ''I'll admit I'm a little nervous about becoming a mother. I used to baby-sit when I was a teenager, so I'm used to children. But being on call twenty-four hours a day is a big responsibility. The baby will be depending on me for everything.''

''If anyone can do it, you can, Rowena. You're the most accomplished woman I know. An actress. A barber. A great cook. I'm sure you'll be a wonderful mother.''

She blinked at the unexpected compliment. ''Thank you.''

''If you're free for lunch today, I'd love to take you out. It's the least I can do after that delicious dinner last night.''

"I'm sorry, Alan, but I have a Sweetheart Dance committee meeting right after church today and I'm not sure how long it will last."

He gave her a crooked smile. "Sweetheart Dance?"

"It's an annual Valentine's Day dance sponsored by the Cooper's Corner chamber of commerce. All ages are welcome to attend."

"And you're on the committee?"

"One of six volunteers to organize and decorate," she replied. "Plus, I donate a free hairstyle and makeup session for the winner of the raffle. Almost everyone in town will be there."

"Do you have a date?"

Wings of panic fluttered in Rowena's chest. Was he about to ask her out? "No."

"Do you want one?"

A dangerous question. One she couldn't afford to answer the wrong way. She found Alan attractive. But just because he'd changed his attitude toward her didn't mean she could trust him.

She had to put her baby's best interests first. And no matter how much Alan appealed to her as a man, she still feared that shuttling her baby back and forth between two homes—and two countries—would leave emotional scars that could last a lifetime.

"I think I'll just go stag again this year," she said at last. "I'm usually too busy with committee work to dance, anyway."

He nodded, then stood up to take his leave. If he was disappointed by her answer, he didn't show it. "Thanks again for the hot chocolate, Rowena."

"Thank you for clearing the sidewalk."

"I'd still like to take you out for lunch," he said. "If you're not free today, how about tomorrow?"

She shook her head. "I'll be busy all day tomorrow."

"But you have to eat sometime," he persisted. "I can bring lunch to the barbershop if it's more convenient for you."

Rowena set down her cup. "That's very thoughtful of you, Alan, but tomorrow just won't work for me."

"I thought we had a truce." He shrugged into his coat and pulled out his gloves. "But now I'm getting the distinct feeling you're trying to brush me off."

"It's not that," she said hastily. "I really do have a meeting today. And tomorrow I need to be in Williamstown for a one o'clock appointment." She hesitated, then told him the truth. "With my doctor."

"Really?" His gaze dropped to her stomach, well concealed by her oversize sweatshirt. "Is something wrong?"

"No. I'm perfectly fine." She rose to her feet. "This is just a routine prenatal visit. I'm supposed to go once a month."

"Why?" he asked, appearing truly curious. "What do they check?"

"Why don't you come with me," she suggested impulsively, "and find out for yourself?"

ON MONDAY AFTERNOON, Rowena sat in Dr. Milburn's waiting room, hoping she hadn't made a big mistake. She could have kicked herself yesterday for inviting Alan to come along with her on this appointment. But the more she thought about it, the more she tried to convince herself this was a smart move.

Especially when she saw Alan seated in the chair beside her, looking distinctly uncomfortable in the crowded waiting room. Two small children shrieked as they chased each other around the chairs, while a baby cried inconsolably in his mother's arms. Their discussion yesterday morning about the demands of a baby had seemed to catch him off guard. He might even be having second thoughts about pursuing his rights in court.

Alan leaned over and whispered, "Why is it taking so long?"

The spicy scent of his aftershave momentarily made her have second thoughts about turning down his invitation to the dance. "Dr. Milburn usually runs a little late. It's probably difficult for him to schedule appointments around emergencies and deliveries. Babies arrive at all hours of the day and night."

"Are you sure they'll let me go in with you?"

She nodded. "I've seen other men accompany their pregnant wives or girlfriends into the exam room. Although you seem to be the only expectant father here today."

"I noticed," he said wryly, then nodded toward a pregnant woman in the far corner of the room. "I didn't think a stomach could stretch that much."

She smiled. "Maybe she's having twins."

He turned toward her. "What about us? Is that a possibility?"

She was surprised at the spark of hope in his eyes. Maybe he thought twins would be the perfect solution to their problem. One baby for each of them. "I suppose twins are possible, but not very likely. There's no history of multiple births in my family. How about yours?"

He shook his head. "None that I know of. But we can always hope."

His tone more than his words made Rowena wonder if she'd made a crucial error in her strategy. Inviting him along today had been an impulse—a chance to prove to him that she was serious about their truce. Only she hadn't expected him to show so much interest. Or excitement.

A nurse opened the door into the waiting room. "Rowena Dahl?"

"That's us," Rowena said, rising to her feet. "Are you ready?"

"Lead the way," he replied, walking beside her as she followed the nurse.

"Here's our first stop." The nurse led them to a scale. "The least favorite one, according to most of my patients."

"I'm sure it will be mine, too, before all of this is through." Rowena slipped off her shoes and stepped onto the scale.

"Wait until you start sorting through your closet looking for your lightest maternity clothes." The nurse chuckled as she adjusted the weight on the slide bar. "Some women shed all their jewelry, even their eyeglasses, before they'll finally step on the scale."

"Actually, I'm hoping I gained weight this month. It's been fluctuating a little."

"So I see," the nurse said with a slight frown. "You lost a pound."

"Is that bad?" Alan asked, concern etched on his face. "How much is she supposed to gain?"

"A woman who is average weight, like Rowena, should gain about twenty-five to thirty-five pounds throughout the course of a pregnancy."

Rowena could see Alan do a quick calculation in his head.

"So about three and a half pounds per month?"

The nurse shook her head. "Generally, a pregnant woman will gain less than that in the first trimester and more in the second and third. The baby will gain about a pound a week during the ninth month of pregnancy."

Alan scowled. "So why is Rowena losing weight? Are there certain foods she should be eating?"

"This is Alan Rand," Rowena interjected, realizing she probably should have made the introductions earlier. "He's the…father."

"So I gathered." The nurse smiled. "I wish all expectant fathers were this interested in pregnancy. I can give you some informational brochures if you'd like."

Alan nodded. "I'd appreciate that."

The nurse led them to the exam room, where she took Rowena's blood pressure, then handed her a blue paper gown. "You can change into this. Take everything off but your panties. The doctor will be here shortly."

They both watched her leave, then turned to each other.

Alan cleared his throat, his gaze falling to the paper

gown in her hand. "Would you like me to wait outside?"

"No, you can stay here while I just step into the dressing room," she replied, indicating the curtain behind her. If she let him out of her sight he might start interrogating any nurses he came across in the hallway.

"All right."

Rowena slipped into the dressing room and removed her sweater and bra, then draped the paper gown over her shoulders, awkwardly tying it at the neck in the back. Then she slid her black stretch pants off. When the gown was secure, she folded all her clothes into a neat pile and set them on the bench. Then she stepped out of the dressing room and found Alan seated on a chair.

"It's freezing in here." She backed up to the exam table and hoisted herself on to it, her bare feet hanging over the edge. "Of course, I'm only wearing paper."

His gaze slid down her body to her slender bare legs. "I noticed."

The door to the exam room opened, and her physician stepped inside. "Hello, Rowena."

"Hi, Dr. Milburn. This is Alan Rand," she said, motioning to him. "He's the father of my baby."

Dr. Milburn's eyebrows rose. No doubt he was wondering how Rowena had tracked down her mysterious sperm donor. But he recovered nicely and extended his hand. "Nice to meet you, Mr. Rand. And congratulations."

"Thank you." Alan reached out to shake his hand.

"I hope you don't mind if I ask some questions while I'm here. This is all new to me."

"Ask away," Dr. Milburn replied. Then he turned to Rowena, who lay on the exam table, and gently palpated her abdomen. "So how have you been feeling, Rowena?"

"Just fine. A little more tired than usual."

"That's normal. Any nausea?"

"A little. Sometimes the odor of frying food bothers me. Especially greasy food."

"You should stay away from that anyway," Dr. Milburn replied, helping her to a sitting position.

"I'll see to it," Alan informed him.

She smiled at his solemn tone. Alan made it sound like she was a bomb destined to blow at any moment. No doubt she'd look like one before long.

"You mean no more French fries or mozzarella sticks?" She shook her head. "Sorry, guys, I don't think I can do it. Those are my comfort foods."

"As long as you eat them in moderation." Dr. Milburn jotted a few notes in her medical chart. "Everything looks good today. We'll schedule an ultrasound next month and take your baby's first picture."

"An ultrasound?" Alan asked, his brow furrowed. "Is there a problem?"

"No, ultrasound is pretty much a standard diagnostic tool. It provides a safe, noninvasive and accurate investigation of the fetus."

"What exactly do you need to investigate?"

"Quite a few things, Mr. Rand," Dr. Milburn replied. "The size of the baby. Placental location. The possibility of multiple births. The sex of the baby.

Although that can be somewhat tricky, depending on the baby's position in the uterus at the time of the test. Which brings up a good question. Will you two want to know the sex when we do the ultrasound?''

Alan looked at her. "Do we?"

She shook her head, wondering if he planned to stick around that long. Surely he had to go back to Toronto sometime. "I think I'd rather be surprised.''

"That's fine." The doctor reached for Rowena's file. "Just be sure and tell the technologist that before the test so she doesn't let something slip.''

"I will," Rowena said, adjusting the paper gown around her hips.

"Now," Dr. Milburn said with a twinkle in his green eyes, "how would you like to hear your baby's heartbeat?''

"So soon?" Rowena asked in wonderment.

Dr. Milburn nodded as he moved to the cupboard behind him. "We use something called a Doppler. It's a fetal stethoscope with a transducer that amplifies sound.''

Alan reached for her hand as the doctor returned to the exam table with the Doppler. He smoothed some clear gel over Rowena's slightly rounded stomach, then slowly slid the sensitive instrument over her skin.

"There it is," Dr. Milburn said at last. A rhythmic, amplified *whoosh, whoosh, whoosh* filled the air.

Alan swallowed hard as he stared at her stomach. "That's the baby?''

She nodded, tears pricking her eyes. "It's the most beautiful sound I've ever heard.''

"It's…incredible," Alan breathed. Then he lifted

his gaze and looked at her in a way that made her breath catch. "Thank you."

"For what?" she asked softly.

"For letting me come here with you today." He cleared his throat. "And for having my baby."

Rowena blinked back her tears and tried to harden herself to the sight of a father's love blossoming before her eyes. But it was too late.

Alan Rand had already found his way into a tiny corner of her heart.

CHAPTER ELEVEN

ALAN STEERED his car onto the highway and headed back toward Cooper's Corner. "I still can't get over it. I've never heard anything like that before. There's a real live person inside of you."

She looked out her window at the passing scenery as trepidation filled her. If only she didn't feel so torn by his enthusiasm. Sharing that moment together threw her completely off balance. She'd been so certain before that keeping this baby for herself was the right thing to do. Now she wasn't sure of anything anymore.

A light sleet began to fall, the tiny ice crystals tapping against the windshield.

Alan flipped on the wipers. "I'm concerned about your weight, though. You have to start eating more, Rowena. How about if you let me cook you supper tonight?"

She swallowed a sigh of frustration. Why did he have to be so considerate? What had happened to the old controlling Alan?

He fell in love with his baby.

She shook that thought from her mind. "You don't have to cook for me, Alan. I plan to start eating more."

"But you told the doctor the smell of food cooking makes you sick."

"Only every once in a while. If I avoid frying foods, especially meat, I'll be fine."

"How about pizza?" he asked. "We could pick one up before we leave town. Does that sound good to you or is it too spicy?"

"It's too much trouble," she told him. "I was just planning to warm up some vegetable soup when I got home."

He frowned. "That's not going to help you gain weight. You're already behind schedule."

That made her smile. "I'm not behind schedule. Dr. Milburn wasn't the least bit worried. But I promise to start eating more if it will make you feel better."

"It will," he assured her. "And I think you should cut back on work, too."

"Alan," she admonished, her amusement turning to exasperation. He was taking this father-knows-best routine a little too far. "I have steady customers. I can't let them down."

"I understand. My mother was a hairdresser."

She nodded. "That's right. The first time we met you told me you'd practically grown up in her beauty shop."

"She shared the shop with my aunt in the basement of our home. Along with a string of steady customers for over twenty-five years." A reminiscent smile haunted his lips. "I never had to pay for a haircut until five years ago. Mom always wanted to do it for me."

Something in his tone made her throat tight. "You must have loved her very much."

He nodded, his gaze fixed on the sleet-covered road in front of him. "So, have you ever thought about hiring extra help at your shop? Maybe even going into partnership with another barber?"

"I like things just the way they are," she replied, watching the way his broad hand rested lightly on the steering wheel. His fingers were long and solid, the nails clean and blunt-tipped. For an insane moment, she wondered how they'd feel against her bare skin.

"But wouldn't it be nice to have a backup? Someone you can call on if you're not feeling well?"

"I suppose," she agreed, then grinned. "But what if I hired a hairdresser who's even better than me? She might decide to open her own shop in Cooper's Corner. Then I'd be guilty of training my competition."

"Yeah, but after the baby's born, you'll have to quit anyway."

She blinked at him in surprise. "Quit? Are you serious? Haven't you ever heard of a mother working outside the home before?"

"Sure," he replied, flipping up the windshield wipers another notch as more sleet began to fall. "But I don't want my baby raised in a day-care center with a bunch of other kids."

She clenched her jaw at his proprietary tone. "I'll agree that in a picture-perfect world, it's best if the mother can stay home with her baby. But that's not always a choice."

"I believe if something is important enough, then

you can find a way to make it work. As a matter of fact,'' he continued, ''I've been giving some thought to this very issue. Speaking hypothetically, do you think you could be happy living in Toronto?''

She stared at him. ''Why?''

''Why not? It's a beautiful, culturally diverse city. We've got the Canadian Opera Company and the National Ballet. Plus the third largest theater venue in the world, after New York and London.''

''Toronto is great,'' she agreed. ''But my home is here. So is my business.''

''The great thing about your business,'' he said, ''is that you can locate anywhere. So why not Toronto? Then our baby can have both parents in the same city. You could stay with the baby during the day while I work, then I'll take over while you work. It's the perfect setup.''

''Since we're speaking hypothetically,'' she said, her ire rising at the way he was trying to rearrange her life like pieces on a game board, ''what do you think about moving to Cooper's Corner?''

He snorted. ''With a population of less than a thousand people? As much as I like it, Cooper's Corner is hardly the capital of the publishing world.''

''Does it need to be? With the Internet and e-mail and fax machines, technology has made it possible to work almost anywhere.''

He shook his head. ''I think it makes more sense to have the baby grow up in Toronto.''

Rowena wished she could argue with him, but he was right. She had enough money from her career as a soap opera actress that she didn't need to work. And it *would* be better for their baby if both parents lived in the same city. She'd been so concerned about the prospect of shuttling her child back and forth across the border that she hadn't considered the most obvious solution.

Still, something rankled inside her that Alan assumed she'd just pick up her life at the snap of his fingers and start all over again. Leave her home. Her business. Her friends. Of course, none of those things were as important as her baby.

"I know it's a lot to ask," Alan began, his tone more conciliatory. "But if you—"

His words were cut off as a small car in the opposite lane lost control on the slick highway and crossed the center line. A scream ripped from Rowena's throat as Alan slammed on the brakes. The Mustang spun out of control on the ice, barely missing the car in front of them.

"Hold on!" Alan shouted as their car careened off the highway and into a ditch. It stopped with a hard jolt against a steep snowbank.

For a moment, Rowena couldn't hear anything except the thundering beat of her heart.

Alan turned to her, his hand on her shoulder, his brown eyes full of concern. "Are you all right?"

She gave him a shaky nod. "Yes, I think so. How about you?"

"I'm fine." Then he slammed his open palm against the steering wheel. "What an idiot! He could have killed us back there."

"He looked like a kid." She craned her neck toward the highway. "What happened to him?"

"He didn't even stop," Alan replied, his nostrils flaring.

"So now what? Can we get out of here?"

"I'm about to find out." He slipped off his seat belt and reached for the door handle. The door was blocked by the snow and only opened a few inches. He pivoted on the seat, then used both feet to pry it open before climbing out.

Cold air swirled into the car. Rowena's lower back began to tighten, and she wondered if she'd strained it somehow in the accident. She closed her eyes and said a silent prayer of thanks. They'd been so lucky. Their car could have easily collided with the other vehicle when it spun out of control, or even rolled over into the ditch.

A moment later, Alan climbed into the car and closed the door. "We're definitely stuck. I'll need to call a tow truck."

A strange tightening sensation banded around her lower abdomen. She reached out to grip the armrest against the pressure.

"Rowena?" Alan looked at her, his brown eyes bright with concern. "What's wrong?"

She swallowed hard as tendrils of panic licked at her, making it difficult to speak. "I'm not exactly sure. You'd better call an ambulance, Alan. I think something might be wrong with the baby."

She saw her fear reflected in his eyes. Then he hastily pulled his cell phone from the pocket of his coat and punched out 911.

"Come on," he muttered. "Come on. Answer."

Rowena closed her eyes as Alan finally began speaking to an operator.

"We need an ambulance," he said, his heart beating so fast he found it hard to breathe.

"Your name, please," the operator asked, "and the nature of your emergency?"

"Alan Rand. We've been involved in a car accident on Highway Seven. About fifteen miles south of Williamstown. You have to hurry. There's a pregnant woman here who needs to see a doctor immediately."

"Is she—" The operator's voice was cut off by a burst of static.

"What?" Alan cried. "I can't hear you."

The static cleared. "Is she conscious?"

"Yes."

Rowena shifted on the seat as the strange achy cramp finally subsided. She moved slightly to see if the motion caused her further pain. "I think I'm all right now, Alan. It went away."

He placed his palm over the mouthpiece of the phone as he turned to her. "I'm not taking any chances. You still should see a doctor."

She wasn't about to argue with him. Rubbing her hands up and down her coat sleeves, she suppressed a shiver. "It's freezing in here."

He shrugged out of his jacket as he propped the phone against his shoulder. "Please hurry," he told the operator. "She's barely four months pregnant."

"Calm down, sir," the operator calmly entreated. "And please stay on the—" Another burst of static cut off her words. Alan swore as he switched off the cell phone then tossed it aside.

"I know you're cold," he said, sliding closer to her and draping his jacket over her. "But we can't turn on the heat. The exhaust pipe is buried too deep in the snowbank to risk switching on the ignition. Carbon monoxide fumes would back up into the car."

"Please put your coat back on." Rowena suppressed another shiver. "I don't need it. You'll die of pneumonia."

"You should be so lucky," he teased.

Another cramp tightened across her abdomen, and a low moan escaped from deep in her throat. She grabbed for his hand. "Alan, I think I'm in labor."

"It's too soon."

"I know, but these must be contractions. How do I—" her voice caught as another spasm gripped her "—make them stop?"

"I don't know." He circled his arm around her. "The ambulance is on its way. Just hold on."

Panic seized her. "What if it's not here soon enough? What if…"

"Shhh," he murmured, pulling her closer until her head lay on his shoulder. The heat of his body surrounded her like a cocoon. "Our baby is strong. You heard the heartbeat today. And he's stubborn, too, like both of us."

"The contraction is fading now." She licked her dry lips, then took another deep, gulping breath. "Alan, I am so scared."

"I know," he said, his breath feathering through her hair. "So am I."

It was true. Alan had never felt so helpless in his life. He was a man used to taking charge. The day he'd been diagnosed with Hodgkin's disease, he'd gone out to research the latest treatments. He'd started a new diet and exercise program, willing himself back to health. But now all he could do was wait and hope and pray.

For the baby they both wanted so much.

He placed his hand on her sweater, gently smoothing it over her slightly swollen belly. "I never wanted to become a father this way, Rowena. I was mad as hell when I found out about the mistake at the Orr Clinic. But after hearing the heartbeat today..." His voice trailed off, then he gazed into her eyes. "I can't imagine my life without the baby."

"Why is this happening?" she asked, her voice choked.

"I don't know." He wrapped her in his arms, wishing he could take away her pain. "But I don't think I realized how much I wanted this baby until right at this moment."

Snow began to fall, swirling around the car. He glanced at his watch. Fifteen minutes had gone by since the accident. Where the hell was that ambulance?

"Here comes another one," she gasped.

He watched her flawless features contort with pain, and another wave of helplessness washed over him. Alan had come to Cooper's Corner to handle this situation. But nothing could have prepared him for this. If Rowena lost the baby now... No, he wouldn't even let himself consider that possibility.

He reached for her hand, threading his fingers

through hers. "Hang on to me, Rowena. And squeeze as hard as you want."

She groaned in response, her eyes closed. Her fingers tightened around his hand, and Alan wished he could do more. He'd never felt so powerless in his life.

"This isn't right," she cried after the contraction had passed. "I can't have the baby yet."

"I know," he murmured, cradling her head against his shoulder. "But you need to stay calm."

"I'm in labor! And I'm only in my fourth month. I could lose this baby, Alan." She choked on the words. "How can I stay calm?"

He grasped her chin and turned her face to his. "Because I know you can. Our baby needs you to be strong. You have to fight as hard as you possibly can."

"I will," she promised, tears glittering in her lashes. "I'll do anything for this baby."

"I know you will." He wrapped her in his arms, wishing he could protect them both from the fear that was coiled around his heart. "And I know, at this moment, I wouldn't want any other woman carrying my child."

Before she could respond, another contraction stole her breath away.

"Hold on," he said, glancing at his watch again. The contractions were about six minutes apart. Was that good or bad?

Dumb question. Any contraction at this stage of the pregnancy had to be bad.

At last, the tension lines around her mouth eased

and she slumped against him, the hair on her brow damp with perspiration. "What if the ambulance can't find us?"

"They'll find us," he said firmly, willing it to be so. "I've got the hazard lights flashing on the car. But if you want, I can go up on the highway and flag it down."

"No," she said, grabbing his jacket when he started to move. "Please stay here with me."

Hearing the entreaty in her voice, he settled her against him once more, brushing a stray curl off her cheek. He had to help her stay calm. The best way to do that was to concentrate on the future instead of the ominous present. "So do you think our baby is a boy or a girl?"

"I don't know," she said, her voice raw. "Which do you want?"

He spoke in a low, soothing tone. "Either one would make me happy. Although I'm still partial to the name Ulysses Herman Rand."

That brought a smile to her pale lips. "The perfect name for a prime minister."

"Or a president." Alan brushed his lips against her temple. "It seems a little silly now, doesn't it? The way we've been fighting over this baby. I'm sorry if anything I've done has caused this to happen."

"No," she assured him. "This isn't your fault. I'm the one who is sorry. I should have rescheduled my doctor's appointment when I heard the forecast. I was just so anxious...."

"I know," he murmured. "Me, too. But we can't

start blaming ourselves. Neither one of us can see into the future.''

That was what scared her. Hot tears seeped from her eyes as she admitted to herself that she might lose this baby. If the doctors couldn't stop the contractions… No, she wouldn't let herself even think it. Alan was right. She had to stay strong. Had to find a way to hold on.

ALAN WATCHED Rowena take a deep, calming breath and couldn't help but admire her courage. Many women would be hysterical by now. Hell, *he* was feeling a little hysterical.

Pain flashed in her eyes. ''Here comes another one.''

The contractions were five minutes apart now. ''Look at me,'' he commanded, his broad fingers lightly squeezing her hand.

She lifted her amethyst gaze to his. He could see tears gleaming in her eyes, but she rapidly blinked them back. ''Now take a slow, deep breath and picture our baby on her first birthday.''

''You…think it's going to be…a girl?''

''I hope so,'' he replied. ''Especially if she's as beautiful as her mother. Can you see her in your mind? She has your amazing eyes.''

''And your dark hair,'' Rowena gasped, wishing with all her heart that it would really happen.

''She's wearing a party hat and digging her fingers into the frosting on her cake.''

''What kind…of cake?''

"Chocolate cake with white frosting and a big pink polka-dot candle."

"I want to get her the purple giraffe," Rowena said, the tears spilling onto her cheeks. "The one I saw at the general store."

"I'll buy it today," Alan promised, his voice strained. "She'll be the happiest birthday girl ever."

"Please let it come true," Rowena prayed, her eyelids shuttered as the contraction finally reached its peak, then slowly faded.

A siren shrieked in the distance, and Rowena almost wept with relief.

"It will happen, Rowena," Alan said. "I promise."

CHAPTER TWELVE

ALAN PACED outside the emergency room of the North Adams Regional Hospital. The ambulance had brought Rowena in over three hours ago, and he still had no word on her condition.

What if she'd lost the baby? He kept replaying the accident over and over in his mind. Why hadn't he slowed down? Why hadn't he seen that car coming sooner? But he knew the answer, and guilt washed over him. *Because he'd let himself get distracted by his sell job to convince Rowena to move herself and the baby to Toronto.*

Now there might not be a baby.

He knew such an outcome would have probably been a relief to him when he'd first come to Cooper's Corner. That thought made him feel sick inside. He hated this sense of being out of control. It had happened first when he was diagnosed with cancer. Then when he discovered his sperm had been used against his knowledge—and against his will. Now this.

But once he'd heard the heartbeat, the baby had suddenly become real for him. Until today, he'd thought of this child as an obligation he had to fulfill. A chance to prove that he could be a good father, unlike his dad. He'd been looking at Rowena's pregnancy from a purely selfish point of view. How it would affect *his* life. How *he* wanted to handle the situation with the least inconvenience to himself.

That wasn't the kind of father he wanted to be.

"Mr. Rand." He looked up to see Dr. Milburn standing in front of him. He'd been at the hospital for a delivery when his office had paged him about Rowena.

"How is she?"

"Rowena is fine. So is the baby. We've managed to stop the contractions."

"Thank God," Alan breathed, slumping against the wall.

"I still want her to stay in the hospital, at least overnight, so I can monitor her condition."

"Are you sure the baby's all right?"

"Yes," Dr. Milburn replied. "We're fairly certain the trauma of the accident triggered the contractions. But fortunately, the membranes didn't rupture, and the placenta is still intact. Rowena will have to stay in bed at home, at least for a little while. But I think she and the baby will both be just fine."

"Can I see her?"

The doctor nodded. "She's been transferred upstairs to the maternity floor. As soon as she's settled into her room, you can go in and see her."

"Thank you, Dr. Milburn." Alan barely restrained from hugging the man. His baby was still alive. He closed his eyes and said a silent prayer of thanks.

Twenty minutes later, Alan stood outside the door to Rowena's hospital room, holding a bouquet of peach roses. His hands were as sweaty as those of a kid on a first date. He took a deep breath, then tapped gently on the hospital door.

"Come in." The sound of Rowena's voice soothed his ravaged nerves.

He walked inside the room. "Hello, beautiful."

A smile curved her lips. "The baby is fine."

"I know. Dr. Milburn told me." He held out the flowers. "I brought these for you."

"They're lovely," she said, taking the bouquet from him and inhaling the delicate blossoms. "And such an unusual color."

"They reminded me of our dinner together the other night." He pulled up a chair. "When I couldn't get enough of your peach cobbler."

Or of looking at you.

She gazed at him with tired eyes. "A lot has happened since then."

He nodded. "More than I ever imagined."

She turned to place the flowers on the table beside her. "I'll have to ask the nurse for a vase to put these in."

"I should have thought of that." He leaned forward, struggling to find the right words. "I should have thought of a lot of things, Rowena. Like how my sudden appearance in Cooper's Corner might affect your condition. Your life. And today…" He shook his head. "When I think about what could have happened…"

She reached out and placed her hand on his forearm. "But it didn't, Alan. Thanks to you. If you hadn't come with me today…" She shivered. "I don't want to even think about what might have happened if I'd been alone in that ditch.''

He scooted his chair closer to the hospital bed. ''Are you sure you're both okay?''

''Positive,'' she assured him. ''In fact, this baby is making its presence known.''

His brow furrowed as he looked at her stomach under the bedcoverings. ''What do you mean?''

''See for yourself.'' She pushed down the sheet, then brought his hand to her stomach. The warmth of her skin permeated through the thin cotton hospital gown she wore.

Then something rippled lightly across his palm. ''That's the baby?'' he asked in amazement.

Her smile widened as she nodded. ''I felt the baby move for the first time a few days ago. But now he or she is causing quite a ruckus in there. Maybe the baby heard us considering the name Ulysses.''

Alan laughed, surprised that he still could after what they'd just been through. ''Hey, that was your idea, not mine.'' His hand smoothed gently over her stomach. ''There he goes again!''

''Feel better?'' she asked.

''Much.'' Then he leaned forward and kissed her. It was a gentle kiss. A kiss of apology. Of gratitude. A kiss that evolved into something more as she parted her lips and let his tongue mate with hers.

Her hand cradled his cheek as she molded her lips to his mouth. Alan basked in the warmth and softness of her. This seemed so natural. So right.

''Hey, you two,'' a nurse called cheerfully as she walked into the room. ''That kind of behavior is frowned upon in the maternity ward. It leads to over-crowding.''

Alan pulled abruptly away from Rowena, wondering what had just happened. Rowena didn't meet his gaze as two pink spots blossomed in her cheeks.

''So how are you feeling?'' the nurse asked, checking the IV. Then she grinned. ''Or do I need to ask?''

''Better,'' Rowena replied, then motioned to the flowers. ''Do you know where I can get a vase?''

''We've got some in the supply closet. I'll bring one in on my next rounds.'' Then she turned to look at the food tray on Rowena's bedside cart and lifted the lid off the plate. ''I see you didn't touch your supper, young lady.''

''I wasn't hungry,'' Rowena said, her gaze flicking to Alan and then away again. ''It's been an eventful day.''

''I know, hon,'' the nurse replied with a sympathetic smile. ''But you still need to eat. How about if I leave the pudding here in case you want a snack later?''

''Wonderful idea,'' Alan interjected. ''I'll make sure she eats it.''

The nurse winked at him. ''If she still won't eat, just threaten not to kiss her anymore.''

Alan looked at the mother of his child. ''Do you think that will work?''

Rowena's blush deepened. ''Sounds like blackmail to me.''

The nurse walked to the door. ''I'll be back to check on you in about twenty minutes. And I'll bring a vase.'' She disappeared, then stuck her head inside a moment later. "By the way, visiting hours are over in five minutes. But good kissers have a twenty-four-hour pass around here."

"How about bad kissers?" Alan asked.

The nurse chuckled. "If you were a bad kisser, I don't think Rowena would be on the maternity ward."

Alan turned to the bed after the nurse left. "It looks like you're in good hands."

She tucked her hair behind one ear. "You're probably tired, Alan. You don't have to stay here."

"Do you want me to leave?"

"No," she replied truthfully.

"Good." He leaned back. "Because this chair is very comfortable."

She laughed. "Liar."

He cleared his throat, hoping she wouldn't take offense at what he was about to propose. "Like I said, you're in good hands here, but what about when you go home? The doctor told me he'll be ordering complete bed rest for at least the next few days."

She tipped up her chin. "I'll stay in bed for the next five months if it means I can have a healthy baby."

He nodded. "The fact is that you'll need someone to take care of you. I'd like to volunteer for the job."

She hesitated. "Alan..."

"I know we didn't get off to the best start," he interjected, before she could turn him down flat. "But I think our truce is going pretty well. I'm a fairly competent cook and I can keep your house running smoothly until you're up and about again."

She licked her lips. "I'm not sure...."

He stopped her words with one hand. "I'd really like to do this, Rowena." Now that he'd made the offer, he couldn't bear the thought of her turning him down. "For you. For our baby."

She leaned against the pillow with a sigh. "I promise to make a lousy patient."

He grinned. "My favorite kind."

She shook her head. "I hope you know what you're getting into, Mr. Rand."

"I think I do," he said huskily. Then he turned and picked up the bowl of pudding the nurse had left on the table. "Now, are you ready to try a bite?"

She grimaced. "I know I should eat something, but I'm really not hungry."

"But the baby must be. Maybe that's why he's so active tonight. Tapioca is probably one of his favorites."

"Okay." She surrendered with a sigh. "I'll try a couple of bites."

"See, you're not such a lousy patient after all." He peeled off the plastic wrap and dipped the spoon into the creamy pudding. Then he placed it in front of her mouth. "Ready or not, baby, here it comes."

She arched a brow. "I'm perfectly capable of lifting a spoon, Alan."

"The doctor said you were supposed to rest. Besides, this makes me feel useful."

She hesitated a moment, then dutifully opened her mouth and let him slip the spoon inside.

"Well?" he asked.

She wrinkled her nose. "It's awful."

He took a small taste, then tried not to grimace.

"It's no peach cobbler. But I bet our baby loves it." Then he dipped up another spoonful and held it out to her.

"I think the baby would rather have chocolate," Rowena said before taking another bite.

"You can have chocolate tomorrow," he promised. He'd promise her anything just to see another smile.

"If I'm lucky, I'll be out of here by tomorrow."

"Then we'll have chocolate at home."

Home. It seemed so natural for him to say it. But his home was in Toronto. This arrangement between them couldn't last forever.

Could it?

For the first time, Alan wondered why he'd never considered a future with Rowena. Not just living in the same city, but the same house. It would solve a lot of their problems. Besides, they liked each other. Respected each other. And if that kiss had been any indication, there was potential for so much more if they just gave their relationship a chance to grow.

He dipped up another spoonful of pudding, then held it out to her. But her eyes were closed, and her head was tilted back on the pillow.

"Rowena?" he said softly, wondering if she was faking just to get out of finishing her tapioca. But the dark shadows under her eyes convinced him she was exhausted.

He quietly set the bowl of pudding on the bedside table, then leaned across her to turn off the light. Even after all that had happened today, she still smelled like gardenias.

Alan slumped down in the chair, exhaustion seeping

into his bones. He narrowed his gaze, watching her in the shadows. It amazed him that just a few weeks ago he'd never known this woman existed. Now she was carrying his child.

And changing his life forever.

ROWENA AWOKE early the next morning as the first rays of dawn began to creep through the window. She turned to see a new nurse standing at her bedside, checking the IV bag.

"I didn't mean to wake you," the nurse whispered, then motioned to where Alan slept awkwardly in the chair. "He's been up half the night, just watching you. He obviously loves you a lot."

Rowena nodded, but she knew the truth. He loved the baby. With each passing day, the child became more real to him. Like yesterday, when he'd talked about the first birthday party. How could she deny him fatherhood?

How could she fit him into her life?

She sighed, pushing the dilemma out of her mind. The scent of roses made her turn toward the bedside table, and she saw the bouquet he'd given her sitting in a green glass vase. Right next to the small bowl of tapioca pudding he'd tried to feed her last night. Two examples that proved Alan Rand wasn't the tyrant she had so desperately wanted him to be.

Struggling to sit up in the bed, she placed her hand on her stomach. Thankfully, there had been no more contractions during the night. In fact, she couldn't remember the last time she'd slept so well. Maybe tapioca pudding had a sedating effect.

Or Alan's kiss.

Only it hadn't made her sleepy. It had made her feel cherished. Desired. Loved.

She turned her head slightly to study him as he slept, noting the dark shadow of whiskers on his jaw and his tousled brown hair. He looked even more handsome than he had the day he'd walked into her barbershop.

But they'd known each other such a short while. Could she risk giving her heart to a man who was practically a stranger? Even if he was the father of her baby. Rowena leaned against the pillow, telling herself she wasn't in any condition to make a major decision. Not only was she physically exhausted, she was emotionally drained, as well.

She yawned, then closed her eyes. Sleep was a peaceful haven where she could dream about Alan without worry. She needed time to sort out her feelings.

Time to figure out what she really wanted.

WEDNESDAY MORNING, Rowena found herself in Alan's arms.

"Don't you think this is a little extreme?" she asked as Alan carried her through the house and into her bedroom.

"The doctor ordered complete bed rest for the next ten days," he replied. "That's the only reason he agreed to release you from the hospital today. I probably shouldn't have let you walk from the car to the front door."

She gave up trying to reason with him. "A girl

could get used to this kind of attention, you know,'' she said, leaning against his chest and letting herself enjoy the moment. ''As well as lose all muscle tone in her body.''

''You feel all right to me,'' he said, laying her gently on her bed. Then he tugged on his shirt collar. ''In fact, I need a cold drink. Would you like something?''

''I think I'll take a bath,'' she said, ready to luxuriate in a tub full of warm water. ''If you promise not to carry me there.''

He frowned. ''I think we forgot to ask the doctor about baths.''

Rowena found that hard to believe. Alan had interrogated poor Dr. Milburn for over thirty minutes this morning about everything she could and couldn't do. The doctor had said she could walk to the bathroom or to the kitchen for a glass of water, but Alan seemed to think her feet shouldn't be allowed to touch the floor.

Time to set him straight.

''Surely Dr. Milburn would have said something if baths were forbidden.''

Alan moved toward the door. ''I'm going to call him anyway, just to be sure. So don't move.''

She leaned against the pillows with a sigh. At least he hadn't resorted to tying her to the bed. But as much as she chafed at the restrictions, she understood his concern. She didn't want to do anything to bring on more premature labor contractions. If that meant letting Alan spoil her rotten, then she'd just have to endure it.

Ten minutes later, he was back in her room carrying a tray. "I talked to Dr. Milburn's nurse, and she told me a bath was fine. And she agreed with me that it wouldn't hurt you to gain a little more weight. So I brought you a snack."

She looked at the tray. It was full of chocolate. Chocolate fudge brownies, chocolate milk and chocolate-iced doughnuts. In the corner of the tray sat a small stuffed pink lamb.

"What's this?" she asked, hearing a rattle when she picked it up.

"The purple giraffe was gone when I got to the store," he said, disappointment in his voice. "I know I promised to get it for you…."

"It's no big deal," she assured him, though she wanted to kick herself for not buying it when she saw it. "This lamb is adorable. Thank you."

"I wasn't sure you'd like it, so I picked up a couple of other stuffed animals while I was there," he said. "Well, six, actually."

"Six?" she echoed with a smile. "Can I see them?"

"Sure." He stood up. "Do you want me to run your bath first?"

She rolled her eyes. "Come on, Alan. I can do that. I'm not completely helpless."

He grinned. "All right. You can run your own bath. But let me know if you want me to scrub your back." Then he turned and walked out of the room, leaving her to stare after him in disbelief.

Was he serious? It would serve him right if she did

call him to come scrub her back. Only he'd probably have the audacity to go through with it. A blush warmed her entire body as she envisioned him doing just that. What was happening between them? Were they actually becoming…friends?

But something told her it was much more than that.

The ring of the doorbell distracted her from embarking down that dangerous line of thinking, and she could barely resist jumping out of bed to answer it. But she knew doing so would only provoke another lecture from Alan. He'd already chastised her once today for pulling on her snow boots.

"You've got a visitor." A feminine voice chimed from the bedroom doorway. She looked up to see Alison Fairchild, her cheeks a rosy red from the winter wind.

"What a nice surprise," Rowena said, sitting up straighter in bed.

"Your butler said I could only stay a minute." Alison grinned as she walked inside the room.

"My butler?" Rowena asked, arching a brow. "Is that what Alan's calling himself now?"

"Not exactly, but he's very efficient. Quite the hunk, too. I definitely want one of those at my house. Where did you find him?"

She swallowed a sigh. "It's a very long story."

"Well, unfortunately, I can't stay long, so you'll have to wait to tell it to me. I just wanted to stop by with your mail," Alison said. "I brought a chicken casserole, too."

"That's so sweet. Thank you."

"I left them both in the kitchen with Alan. Now promise you'll let me know if there's anything else you need."

"Thank you. I will."

Alison hesitated. "I never got a chance to congratulate you, Rowena. I'd heard you were pregnant, but since you hadn't announced it yourself yet, I didn't feel comfortable mentioning it."

"I know," Rowena replied, aware that everyone in town must have a hundred questions about her condition. "It's a little…complicated."

That was the understatement of the century.

"Well, I hope you're back on your feet soon." Alison smiled. "Although I'd certainly enjoy all that undivided male attention if I were you." She reached down to give her a hug. "I think you've found a keeper, Rowena. Congratulations again."

So not only did the people of Cooper's Corner know Rowena was pregnant, but they believed Alan Rand was her lover. She supposed it was only natural, since they knew he was the father of her baby. And explaining the truth to them wasn't something she was prepared to do.

So Rowena pasted a smile on her face the rest of the day as a steady stream of visitors stopped by to see her, delaying her plans for a bath. All her friends and neighbors brought casseroles and small gifts, like books and crossword puzzles to help pass the time she had to spend in bed. They were all delighted and charmed with Alan, too, a few even digging for hints of an upcoming wedding. But she kept her mouth firmly closed on that subject.

At last Alan appeared in her room. "I've put a closed sign on the front door. And your bath awaits, my lady. With lots of bubbles. Would you like me to carry you there?"

"Yes," she replied, more tired than a woman who'd spent the day in bed should be, "but I think I'd better walk anyway."

She threw back the coverlet and climbed out of bed. Alan retrieved her robe from the closet and slipped it over her shoulders. Then he pulled her long blond hair free of the terry-cloth collar.

"Any pain or contractions?" he asked.

"None at all," she replied, cinching the robe's belt loosely around her waist. "I feel as good as new."

"Good. I'll have your supper and your medication ready when you're through with your bath."

She turned to face him. "You're going to end up in bed next to me if you keep up this pace." Her gaze flew to his as she realized what she'd said.

His brown eyes darkened. "I can't think of any place I'd rather be."

The air sizzled between them, and Rowena's heart skipped a beat when he reached out one knuckle and skimmed it over her cheek.

"But we'll talk about that later," he said.

She stared at him, trepidation mingling with desire. After pretending that he was her lover all afternoon, she was finding it hard to remember reality. "I'd better hurry before the bathwater gets cold."

"I'll let you know when supper is ready."

She nodded, then headed for the bathroom. Everything was happening much too fast. There was so much to consider. So much to worry about, when all she really wanted to do was enjoy the moment.

Especially the moments she spent with Alan.

CHAPTER THIRTEEN

ALAN SHOVED the last casserole dish into the refrigerator, amazed that he'd found room for it. When he'd first arrived in Cooper's Corner, he'd been curious about how the people here felt about Rowena Dahl. He had no doubts now.

They loved her.

Since the news had spread about the car accident and her hospital stay, people had been phoning and popping in all day. There was enough food in the house to open a restaurant.

He preheated the oven before sticking one of the covered casseroles inside. Then he began cleaning up the kitchen, blaming his nervous energy on his lack of sleep and trying to ignore the images of her naked body submerged in bath bubbles that kept popping into his head.

His mouth watered as the savory aroma of the casserole filled the air. He turned to wipe crumbs off the kitchen counter, then saw the pile of mail sitting there. The postmistress had been kind enough to bring it so he wouldn't have to leave the house. He idly thumbed through the envelopes, then froze, his gut tightening with anger when he saw the one addressed to Savannah Corrington.

Was it from the same creep as before? Maybe Rowena still regularly received fan mail from other loyal viewers of the show, though she'd never mentioned anything about it. Hardly surprising, since she was one of the most modest women he'd ever met. Even with her breathtaking beauty and her successful acting career, she still shied away from attention.

He turned the letter over, tempted to break the seal and read it. But that would be an invasion of her privacy. Still, he didn't intend to let anything upset her. That had definitely been one of the doctor's orders.

A rustling sound in the hallway made him quickly pull open a kitchen drawer and stuff the letter under the molded plastic silverware tray. Then he closed the drawer before gathering the rest of the mail and placing it in a neat pile on her dinner tray.

"Something smells delicious."

He turned to see Rowena standing in the open doorway to the kitchen. She wore the long terry-cloth robe, her thick hair hanging in damp ringlets over her shoulders.

"What are you doing out here?"

She smiled in a way that made his heart drop to his toes. "I live here, remember?"

"You're supposed to be in bed."

She held up both hands. "I know, but I just wanted to make sure you hadn't remodeled the kitchen or anything. According to the reports I've received, you're the model of organization and efficiency."

"And you're disobeying orders." He walked over to her. "Now, will you go back to bed, or do I have to carry you there?"

Mischief glowed in her amethyst eyes. "Let me think about it for a minute."

"Too late." He bent and swooped her up in his arms.

She gasped, then twined her arms around his neck. "I was just joking, Alan."

"I wasn't," he said, carrying her effortlessly toward the bedroom. "I'm going to make sure you follow the doctor's orders to the letter."

She gazed into his eyes. "I won't do anything to endanger the baby, Alan."

"I know," he said, pushing her bedroom door open with his foot before walking inside. "Maybe I just like having a reason to boss you around."

"Now, that I believe," she replied as he laid her gently on the bed.

He stood leaning over her, his neck still entangled in her arms. "You smell like peaches."

"It's that scented bubble bath you put in the water when you filled the tub."

"I like it," he said huskily, then bent to kiss her parted lips. They tasted even better the second time. She moaned into his mouth as he deepened the kiss, the front of her robe parting as she leaned against the pile of pillows behind her.

Alan followed her, his body half reclined on her bed. Their mouths met and clung, tasted and teased.

She slid one hand over his waist, her fingers skimming the bare skin under his sweater. His fingers trailed down her soft cheek, then traced her delicate collarbone.

He lifted his head a fraction of an inch. "You're so

beautiful,'' he breathed, before kissing her again. He inhaled the scent of peaches and Rowena, a heady combination.

She murmured something against his mouth, and he lifted his head. "What?"

"I'm not sure we should do this," Rowena said softly.

He pulled back, furious with himself for losing control. And for bringing her with him. Then he straightened and stepped away from the bed. "You're right. I'm sorry."

"Don't apologize," she said softly. "I'm as much to blame as you are."

"But the doctor told me not to..."

She arched a brow. "Not to what?"

His cheeks burned. "It doesn't matter."

"I want to know."

"Dr. Milburn said we should refrain from... physical contact."

"You mean sex?"

He met her gaze. "Yes."

Her eyes widened. "You asked him about it?"

"Of course not," he replied, backing away from the bed. "Milburn is the one who brought up the subject."

She pulled the lapels of her robe together. "Then I guess that's another good reason to stop."

Another good reason? What was the first? But he was in no condition to continue this conversation. So he nodded, his body throbbing in protest. "I'll bring in your supper tray."

"Thank you," she said, a blush in her cheeks now, too.

Alan turned and left her bedroom, wondering what the hell had come over him. She hadn't even been out of the hospital for twenty-four hours.

"You're losing it, Rand," he muttered as he pulled the casserole dish out of the oven. He couldn't afford to lose his mind.

Especially when he was in imminent danger of losing his heart.

A WEEK LATER, Rowena lay in her bed flipping through the television channels with the remote control. She practically had the television schedule memorized, but nothing appealed to her anymore.

Her confinement in bed had definitely begun to fray her nerves. She'd snapped at Alan this morning when he'd brought in her breakfast tray, then pretended to be asleep when Father Tom Christen stopped by on his weekly round of visiting homebound parishioners. She still felt guilty about that.

She wanted her life back. She missed the barbershop and her customers. She'd love to stop in at Tubb's Café for lunch. Drive over to New Ashford for a shopping spree. Stop at the ice cream parlor there for a banana split.

Then the baby moved, and her frustrations evaporated. Every movement and tiny kick assured her that the baby was doing well. Despite her impatience, she'd stay in this bed until the middle of summer if it meant her baby would be all right.

A knock sounded on her bedroom door, and she looked up to see Maureen standing there.

"Care for some company?"

"I would love it." Rowena clicked off the television set. "What a nice surprise."

"I'm your official baby-sitter," Maureen told her, taking a seat in the wing chair next to the bed. "Alan called me this morning and asked if I could come and stay with you for a couple of hours while he went shopping."

Rowena frowned. "He didn't say anything to me about it."

"That's odd."

Her frown faded. "Maybe not so odd. I did throw a book at his head this morning when he tried to get me to eat a second bowl of oatmeal. He's probably got cabin fever, too. We've both been stuck in this house together for almost a full week."

Maureen shrugged. "He seemed perfectly cheerful to me."

"I know," Rowena mused. "It gets irritating, doesn't it? He's always smiling."

Maureen's green eyes sparkled. "Gee, I wonder why? Could it be that Alan Rand is falling head over heels in love with you?"

Rowena stared at her friend in disbelief. "You really believe that?"

"Don't you?"

She shook her head. "He's here because of the baby, Maureen. That's all. Although I have to admit he'll make a wonderful father."

"The baby may have been the reason he came to

Cooper's Corner in the first place, but I think you're the reason he's stayed so long.''

''And I think you're a hopeless romantic,'' Rowena said, telling herself not to get her hopes up. Nothing had happened between them since that sizzling kiss a week ago. There was desire between them, she couldn't deny that. But desire didn't equal love.

''I'm just glad someone is staying here with you,'' Maureen said. ''I have to admit I've been worried ever since you got that letter. Have there been any more?''

She shook her head. ''Only the one I showed you. It's very strange.''

Relief softened Maureen's expression. ''Well, I'm glad. When I first heard you were in the hospital, I was afraid Max Heller might have been involved. Especially when someone told me the other driver had fled the scene.''

''They found him,'' Rowena said, smoothing the coverlet over her. ''A teenager from New Ashford who had skipped school that day. He was simply driving too fast on those slick roads and panicked after we went into the ditch.''

''Well, I'm sorry it happened,'' Maureen said, ''but I'm also relieved that Max wasn't involved. And I have a confession to make.''

Rowena looked up at her friend. ''What is it?''

''I contacted a cop I know in New York City and asked him to see what he could find out about Heller.'' She held up both hands before Rowena could protest. ''I know it's none of my business, but I didn't like the sound of that letter.''

"So maybe that's why I've only gotten one letter. Your cop friend probably scared Max off."

Maureen shrugged. "Maybe. Although I haven't heard anything yet. As soon as I do, I'll let you know."

Rowena nodded. "Thank you, Maureen. I really do appreciate it. Although I still think Max is relatively harmless. At least with him, I know what to expect. With Alan, my feelings change from one moment to the next."

"Your feelings about him as the father of your baby?" Maureen asked. "Or as a man?"

"Both." Rowena stared at the ceiling. "I think I might be falling in love with him. I never expected it to happen. I never *wanted* it to happen."

Maureen sat on the edge of the bed. "That's how love works, Rowena. It comes when we least expect it. I think you and Alan make a good couple."

"But we're not just a couple," Rowena countered. "With the baby coming, we're almost a family. An accidental family. So how do I know if Alan is really interested in me or if I'm just part of a package deal? If there was no baby, would he still want me?"

"Would you still want him?" Maureen countered.

"Yes," she said slowly. "I think I would. At least, I'd want the man he's been since the car accident. Not the one I saw as a controlling pain in the butt the first day we met. The problem is that I don't know for certain which one is real."

Maureen gave her a sympathetic pat on the knee. "I think all this worrying is probably making you hungry. How about if I fix us a snack?"

Rowena smiled. "I see Alan left orders to feed me until I grow as round as the Cooper's Corner water tower."

"He might have mentioned something about making sure you keep up your strength."

"Okay, I'll take an apple if there are any left."

"How about a glass of milk to go with it?"

"That would be wonderful. Thanks, Maureen."

Five minutes later, Maureen was back with a sliced apple and a glass of milk on the serving tray. "I've been thinking about what you said and I've come up with a possible solution."

Rowena sat up straighter in bed before taking the tray out of Maureen's hands. "I can't wait to hear it."

"Tell him you'll give him legal rights as the father of your baby."

She gaped at her friend. "What?"

"Don't you see?" Maureen sat on the edge of the bed. "You're afraid the only reason Alan might be romancing you is because he wants access to the baby. If you give him that access, he doesn't have any reason to stick around. Unless he truly wants to be with you."

Rowena picked up an apple slice and bit into it, savoring the tartness on her tongue. "But give him legal rights to the baby? Doesn't that seem a little extreme?"

"You just told me he'll make a wonderful father."

It was true. No matter what happened between them in the future, she did believe Alan would be a positive influence in her baby's life. So maybe her reluctance to tell him that had more to do with protecting her heart than her baby. What if, after she granted him those rights, he just walked away from her? What if all he really wanted was the baby?

It was one more worry to add to her collection.

LATER that afternoon, Alan walked into Rowena's bedroom with his arms full of packages. "Wait until you see what I found for the baby."

"It looks like you cleared out the store," she said as he dumped the bags on the end of her bed. "Is Maureen still here?"

"She just left. I'm sorry I was gone so long. The general store was out of fresh peaches, so I drove to New Ashford." He pulled a tiny yellow sleeper out of a sack. "Isn't this great?"

Rowena arched a brow. "That's the strangest peach I've ever seen."

He grinned. "There was a children's clothing store next to the grocery store there." He folded up the sleeper. "I know it looks small, but the saleslady promised me it was the right size for a newborn."

"That's because she probably knows a sucker when she sees one," Rowena said, reaching out to rub the soft fabric. "But it's very cute."

"I'm glad you like it because I bought one in every color." He reached for another sack and pulled out a stuffed animal. "And look at this."

She couldn't help but smile at the excitement in his voice. "It looks like an orange monkey."

He grinned. "It is. But a very special orange monkey. Just listen." He pushed the monkey's belly, and the music of "Pop, Goes the Weasel" began to play.

"Anything else?" she asked as he sorted through the sacks.

"All kinds of stuff. Bibs, rattles, little undershirts and some booties. And this," he said, reaching into another sack.

She laughed. "A baseball?"

"Hey," he replied, tossing it into the air and catching it with one hand, "a star pitcher can't start too young."

"Which team is she going to pitch for?"

His grin turned sheepish. "Okay, so I might have gone a little overboard."

"A little?" She waved one hand over the items spilled across the bed. "If this is any indication, the baby will be spoiled rotten."

"I'll try to restrict myself to buying one toy a day from now on."

She shook her head. "You're impossible."

"I just want to be a father." He looked at her, his gaze serious. "I know I came on too strong the first day we met."

"You already apologized for that," she interjected.

"I know, but I didn't explain why I was acting like such a jerk," he said. "I was afraid, Rowena. I met an intelligent, headstrong woman that day who was the mother of the only child I might ever have. If it came down to a fight, I wasn't sure I could win."

She wrinkled her brow. "What do you mean, the only child you might ever have? You're a young man, Alan. You could have a dozen children."

A muscle flexed in his jaw. "Do you want to know

the reason I made a deposit at the Orr Fertility Clinic? Because my oncologist recommended it.''

''Oncologist?'' The word sent a shiver through her.

He nodded. ''I was diagnosed with Hodgkin's disease three years ago. The oncologist assured me it was highly treatable, but he told me those treatments might leave me sterile.''

''And did they?''

''I don't know,'' he replied. ''I never went in for the test. I suppose I was afraid to find out. If I have a low sperm count, my chances of ever creating another child aren't good.''

''But the Hodgkin's disease…you're all right now?''

He nodded. ''I'm fine. The cancer is gone.''

Rowena sat for a few moments, trying to absorb what he'd just told her. ''So when the Orr Clinic impregnated me with your sperm, they might have destroyed your chance to have a baby with a woman of your choice.''

He reached for her hand. ''Just the opposite. They created that chance. If it wasn't for the Orr Clinic's mistake, we never would have met.''

Her throat tightened. ''So you're not…sorry?''

He placed his hand on her stomach, drawing a tiny kick from the baby. ''At this moment, I feel like the luckiest guy in the world.''

Tears filled her eyes and spilled over. All this time, she'd been so worried about herself. The chaos this situation had caused in her life. And all the while Alan had known this might be his only chance to have a child.

"Hey," he chided, skimming a tear off her cheek with his knuckle. "I didn't mean to make you cry."

"It's my hormones," she lied. But she couldn't deny the truth any longer.

She was falling in love with him.

CHAPTER FOURTEEN

ALAN SAT impatiently in Dr. Milburn's waiting room, resisting the urge to pace up and down the carpet. As before, he was the only male in the room. His gaze fell on a woman who had to be in the last stages of pregnancy. She looked enormous. And extremely uncomfortable.

He tried to imagine Rowena growing that large and smiled at the image. It was hard to believe that in five short months, he could become a father.

If nothing goes wrong.

He glanced at his watch, wondering what was taking so long. Rowena had been strangely silent on their trip to Williamstown this morning, and he knew she was nervous. Dr. Milburn was going to perform some more tests to make certain the baby was out of danger.

Alan wished he'd gone in the examination room with her. But when the nurse told him Rowena would be having an internal exam, he'd decided to give her some privacy and wait out here. A wait that was lasting forever.

A man entered the office, his gaze scanning the room. Then he walked over and sat down by Alan. "Pretty crowded in here today."

"The doctor had a delivery earlier," Alan replied, "so he's running behind."

"As usual," the man said, leaning back in the chair with a sigh. "This your first time?"

"Yes. How about you?"

The man shook his head. "Fourth. I've got three daughters. We're having a boy this time. My wife's gotten too big to fit behind the steering wheel of our car, so I came to pick her up."

"How do you know it's a boy?" Alan asked.

"Ultrasound." The man unbuttoned his coat. "They've got a machine that can look inside the womb and take a picture of the baby. It all looks like a bunch of fuzz to me, but the technician can tell if it's a boy or a girl."

Alan nodded, remembering that Dr. Milburn had asked if Rowena and Alan wanted to know the sex of the baby. At this point, he didn't care if it was a boy or a girl, so long as it was healthy.

"So are you going to be a coach?" the man asked.

"Coach?" Alan echoed, thinking it was a little early to be planning Little League games even if he had already bought the baby a baseball.

"A Lamaze coach," the man explained. "To help your wife through labor and delivery."

Alan didn't bother to correct the man. "I don't know. She hasn't said anything about it."

"Well, it's an experience, let me tell you." The man laughed. "My wife just about broke all the bones in my hand, she gripped it so hard. But it gets a little easier with each baby. Although my wife might not use the word *easy.*"

Alan turned to him, intrigued. "So how do you know what to do?"

"They have Lamaze classes couples can take where they teach the woman how to breathe and stuff. Tell you what you should pack to take to the hospital. You get to watch a childbirth film, too, that just about sends some men screaming out of the room. But it's all worth it in the end."

Alan slowly nodded, wondering when they'd have to take these classes and how long they would last. He couldn't stay in Cooper's Corner much longer. Especially if he wanted a job waiting for him when he got back to Toronto. And what if Dr. Milburn didn't give Rowena a clean bill of health? What if she needed him to take care of her until the baby was born?

A nurse stepped into the waiting room. "Mr. Rand?"

He looked up, startled from his thoughts. "Yes?"

"Would you come with me, please?"

Alan stood, trepidation filling him. He rounded the chair, stumbling slightly. The man next to him held out his hand.

"Good luck, buddy," he said.

"Same to you," Alan replied, shaking the man's hand before following the nurse down the long hallway.

"Is there a problem?" he asked,

She smiled. "No, Rowena asked me to have you join her in Dr. Milburn's office. He's already examined her and will be in there soon for the consultation."

The nurse stopped in front of a door and swung it open. "Here we are."

"Thank you," Alan said, before joining Rowena inside. She sat in one of the brown leather chairs opposite a massive mahogany desk.

He took the seat next to her. "How are you?"

"Fine," she replied with a reassuring smile. "Dr. Milburn just wanted to wait for a couple of test results before he let me go."

The door to the office opened again, and Dr. Milburn stepped inside.

"Sorry to keep you two waiting."

Alan rose to his feet and shook the doctor's hand. "We're anxious to hear about the tests."

"Of course." Dr. Milburn rounded his desk and sat down. He pulled his bifocals out of the pocket of his lab coat. "Just let me take a look here."

Alan and Rowena exchanged nervous glances as Dr. Milburn studied the chart.

At last the doctor looked at them. "I'm very pleased with your progress, Rowena. I think the danger period is finally over."

Alan breathed an audible sigh of relief. "That's the best news I've heard all day."

"Rowena passed all the tests with flying colors," Dr. Milburn announced. "And since you've reported no new contractions, I believe we can safely assume it was a one-time incident caused by the trauma of the car accident."

"I'm so glad," Rowena replied. "I've been feeling pretty good for the most part."

Dr. Milburn studied her chart. "And gaining weight, too, I see. Good job."

"Anyone would gain weight with Alan offering food every five minutes," she replied with a smile that warmed him from the inside out.

"Well, I'm pleased to see he's taking good care of you."

"So does this mean she's off bed rest?" Alan asked the doctor.

"Absolutely. You can resume your normal activities, Rowena, as long as you don't overdo it."

"Maybe you should define normal activities, Doctor," Alan said, "just so we're both clear."

Dr. Milburn perched on a stool, then turned toward Rowena. "You can work, do light housework, travel, have sexual intercourse and just about anything else you want to do. No skiing or ice skating, though." He grinned. "Those activities will just have to wait until next winter."

But Alan barely heard that last part. He was too focused on the two little words that Dr. Milburn had breezily added to the list of activities.

Sexual intercourse.

A clinical way of saying Alan was free to make love to Rowena. Something he'd dreamed about almost every night since moving in with her. And judging by the deep flush on her cheeks, it was something she was thinking about, too.

"So I'll see you in three weeks," Dr. Milburn said, flipping the chart closed, "for your scheduled sonogram. Until then, I don't anticipate any problems. But give me a call if you have any questions or concerns."

Rowena looked at Alan, obviously waiting for him to pepper the obstetrician with more questions. But he couldn't think about anything at this moment except the possibility of making love to her.

"Thank you, Doctor," she said at last, slipping her purse over her shoulder. "I truly appreciate everything you've done."

"Glad to be of service," he said, shaking Alan's hand on his way out the door. "And happy Valentine's Day."

Rowena turned to Alan once they were alone in the exam room. "Are you ready?"

He blinked, momentarily disconcerted by her question. He'd been ready since that kiss they'd shared in her bed a week ago. "Sure. You wait right here while I go warm up the car."

"Didn't you hear the doctor, Alan?" she teased, following him out of the office. "You don't have to spoil me anymore. I'm perfectly fine."

"What if I like spoiling you?" he asked, taking her arm as they walked outside so she wouldn't slip on the snowy sidewalk.

She smiled. "Then I guess I'll just have to suffer through it."

Neither one of them had talked about how long he'd stay with her. But he wasn't going anywhere until this matter with Heller was put to rest. No doubt his office in Toronto was getting antsy for his return, but surprisingly, Alan didn't miss his work at all. Maybe his boss had been right when he'd suggested Alan might be suffering from burnout.

Rowena settled into the car, moving a little slower

now that her pregnancy was becoming more apparent. He thought she'd never looked as beautiful.

"Whoa," she said, placing her hand on her stomach as he climbed into the driver's seat beside her. "That was quite a kick."

"So the little one woke up," Alan said, gently rubbing his palm over her rounded belly. It seemed like such a natural thing for him to do. "I think the baby's trying to tell me something. Good thing I can decipher Morse code."

She arched a skeptical brow. "Morse code?"

"We've got good father and baby communication." He feigned intense concentration. "Let's see…the first two letters were a B and an A. There's an N, another A, another N and another A."

She laughed. "Banana?"

"Now, wait a minute," he replied. "The kid isn't done. There's an S and a P and an L…." He grinned at her. "I've got it. The baby wants a banana split."

"In February?" she asked, still laughing in spite of herself.

"Hey, someone told me New Ashford has a great ice cream parlor that's open all year long. Why don't we stop there on the way home? Give the baby a treat?"

"No fair blaming it on the baby," she said. "I'm the one who's pregnant, but you're the one with the cravings."

"So how about it?" he asked. "Shall we order a banana split for three?"

She smiled. "It sounds great, but I really should get back to Cooper's Corner. The Sweetheart Dance is tonight, and I've got to give the winner of the raffle her free hairstyle and makeup session.''

"Are you still planning to go to the dance?"

She hesitated for a moment. "If I can find a date. Do you know any eligible bachelors?"

He grinned. "Actually, I do know one guy who might interest you. He's a Canadian who works in the publishing business and he's been taking ballroom dancing lessons for the past six months."

Her eyes widened. "Have you really?"

He nodded. "Absolutely. And they've been almost as awful as the swimming lessons."

She laughed. "You never cease to amaze me."

He looked at her for a long moment while the sizzling tension between them slowly mounted. "The feeling is mutual, Rowena."

She turned from him and cleared her throat. "If we have a date, you'd better take me home so I can get ready."

Alan started the engine, his body making him fully aware that he was more than ready for Rowena.

ALAN HELD ROWENA in his arms on the dance floor in the elementary school gymnasium, wondering if he was dreaming again. Her hair smelled like gardenias, and the soft curves of her body fit perfectly against his own. She wore a killer red dress that dipped low enough in the front to make more than one male eye turn in her direction, yet was loose enough around the waist to conceal her pregnancy.

Beneath red streamers draped over the ceiling, couples young and old filled the dance floor. He saw Keegan Cooper dancing reluctantly with one of the young twins. Maureen was dancing with the other twin riding on her hip. Clint stood on the sidelines manning the punch bowl and talking with Ed Taylor, who wore a threadbare blue suit that had seen better days.

It looked as if the whole town had shown up for the dance, and every one of them had taken note of Alan and Rowena.

"Are they still staring?" Rowena asked, her breath whispering against his neck. The sensation caused heat to sizzle through his body.

"Not as much," he replied, turning his attention to her. "Does it bother you?"

She lifted her face to look at him, and he was struck once again by how damn beautiful she was. "Not at all. But I'd hate for you to feel like you were on display."

"I don't think I'm the one they're looking at," he said, expertly sidestepping another couple. "You look breathtaking tonight."

She smiled. "The women aren't staring at me, Alan. They're probably wondering if you're Fred Astaire's illegitimate son. You're a wonderful dancer."

"Glad to know those lessons are finally paying off."

"You were serious before, about taking dance lessons?"

He nodded. "When I found out I had Hodgkin's disease, I started thinking about all the things I should have done but never found the time for. So I decided to make the time. I wrote up a list of everything I wanted to do and started at the top.'' He gave her a wry smile. ''Some of them turned out to be impossible. Like writing a book.''

''Why is that impossible?'' she asked. ''I would think working in publishing would give you an edge.''

''Maybe,'' he admitted. ''If I ever found time to write. I guess I let too many other things get in the way.'' He grinned. ''All the things on my list.''

Her eyes gleamed with amusement. ''You actually made a list?''

''Three pages long,'' he admitted.

''So what else is on it?''

''A bunch of things that don't seem very important anymore. Like riding in a hot-air balloon and taking scuba diving lessons.'' He hesitated. ''Having a child was on the list, too, but way down at the bottom. I should have realized that it belonged at the top.''

Her grip tightened on him. ''It must have been hard for you.''

He knew she was referring to his bout with Hodgkin's disease, and his throat tightened as the memory of those years came rushing back. ''It seems like a lifetime ago.''

The song ended, and the bandleader announced a fifteen-minute break. Alan and Rowena found two empty chairs in the corner of the gymnasium.

''Would you like some more punch?'' he asked.

She reached for his hand. ''I'd like you to tell me what you went through three years ago.''

He sucked in a deep breath, not certain he was ready to share those feelings he'd tried so hard to bury. But when she gently squeezed his hand, he knew he didn't want to hold anything back from her.

"I think the worst part of it was being alone," he began. "My mom had passed away two years earlier, and my dad…" He cleared his throat. "He wasn't around much."

"I can't imagine a parent not being there for a child at a time like that. Even if that child is an adult."

"I can't, either," he replied honestly. "But my dad was never there for me while I was growing up. I'm not even sure he liked me, much less loved me."

He saw the look of horror on her face. "Hey, don't worry about it. I realized a long time ago that my father and I would never have a relationship. He grew up an orphan, so maybe that's why he could never connect with me. I don't know the reason. All I do know is that I never want my child to wonder if his father cares about him. That's why I'm so determined to be a good father myself."

Rowena slowly nodded. "We've both let our pasts dictate our future. I grew up the child of divorced parents who loathed each other. The problem was that I loved both of them so much I couldn't bear to be part of that animosity. But I didn't have a choice. I don't think they even realized they were using me as a weapon in their battle, but I was the one who almost got destroyed."

He held his breath as she talked, realizing she must trust him to reveal this much of herself.

"I left home as soon as I graduated from high school," she continued, "and landed in New York City. I met a man named Max Heller there. He was handsome, charming and the most sophisticated man I'd ever known.''

He thought about telling her he'd overheard Maureen's telephone call about Heller and the letter. But he decided against it, not wanting to break her flow. ''I hate him already.''

A smile teased her lips. ''He was a director on *Another Dawn,* and I thought he was wonderful. At first. But soon I learned he wanted to direct me offstage as well as on. He wanted to dictate everything I did in my life.''

''I can imagine how well that went over.''

Her smile widened. ''I'm sure you can. Although I wasn't quite as confident in myself back then. I mistook his attention for love. It took me a while to figure out how Max's need to control me wasn't healthy for either of us.''

''So you got away from him.'' It was a statement, not a question.

''Not soon enough.'' She suppressed a shiver. ''I realized how bad it was when I won a role in an off-Broadway play. A role Max hadn't wanted me to take.''

''Why not?''

She shrugged. ''He didn't think the money was good enough. He was furious when I pursued it even after he advised me against it.''

''So what happened?''

''He called the producer of the play and told him I was close to a nervous breakdown and couldn't take on the pressure of another role in addition to playing Savannah Corrington.''

"Don't tell me the producer bought that?"

"He did. Max had called in a favor with a tabloid reporter, so an item about my impending collapse appeared in the paper that same day. I can't really blame the producer. He couldn't afford to take a chance on someone he thought was unstable."

"Heller sounds completely twisted."

She nodded. "He didn't want to just keep me from doing the play. He wanted to humiliate me. To punish me for going against his wishes."

"So that's when you left him?"

"Yes." She leaned back in her chair. "Shortly after that I left show business and moved to Cooper's Corner. And I haven't looked back since."

"Do you miss it?" he asked, truly curious. "The big city? The fame? The glamour?"

"It's a different lifestyle," she admitted. "Some actors become addicted to it. I never did. The business was too cutthroat for me."

"Publishing can be the same way," he replied. "Great highs, but lots of lows, too. I used to love it, but lately I can't seem to dredge up the same drive to succeed that I used to have. Maybe it got zapped away during those radiation treatments."

"Or maybe you just realized what's really important in life."

He looked into her eyes, seeing the most important person to him at this moment. "Maybe you're right."

Phyllis Cooper approached their table. "My, don't you two look serious."

"Hi, Phyllis," Rowena said. "The decoration committee did a wonderful job. The gym looks great."

Phyllis preened. "Why, thank you. I had great people helping me. My Bonnie, of course, Burt Tubb and Alison Fairchild. We all worked hard to make it as romantic as possible. The papier-mâché Cupid hanging over the dance floor was my idea. Sort of like mistletoe at Christmas." Her gaze moved over the couples nuzzling together as they danced. "It seems to be working, too."

Rowena motioned to Alan. "This is my date, Alan Rand. Alan, this is Phyllis Cooper."

Phyllis's eyes twinkled. "We've already met. Mr. Rand has been in my store several times. He's not much of a talker, though."

"I've always been a little shy," Alan confessed, meeting Rowena's amused gaze.

Phyllis nodded with approval. "The strong, silent type. I like that. And I'm so glad to see you here together. I told Philo not to worry about that little tiff you had in the store. You two are such a cute couple that I was sure you'd make up."

Alan saw the flush in Rowena's cheeks. "If you'll excuse us, Mrs. Cooper, I was just about to ask Rowena to dance with me."

"Of course," Phyllis said. "Although I think Cupid's already found his mark with you two."

Rowena's face was as red as her dress by the time they reached the dance floor. "I've never been so mortified in my life. Cupid's already found his mark. Can you believe she actually said that?"

Alan laughed as he pulled her into his arms. "No. But I'm having a great time. How about you? Tired?"

"Maybe a little," she admitted. "It's amazing how

spending ten days in bed can drain a person's energy.''

''Then why don't you let me take you home?''

She circled her arms around his neck. ''First I want to see if that Cupid Phyllis made really works.''

Then she kissed him.

CHAPTER FIFTEEN

TIME STOPPED for Alan when Rowena reached up to kiss him. The dance music and the crowd around them faded away as she moved her soft, succulent lips over his mouth. A low groan rumbled in his chest, and he pulled her closer, relishing the contact of her body against his own.

Alan had kissed women before, but never like this. He poured his heart and soul into it, telling her with his body what he couldn't yet communicate with words. She threaded her fingers through his hair, and the sensation nearly destroyed him. His body throbbed with desire. And from the soft, needy whimpers he heard emanating from her throat, that desire was mutual.

"Ladies and gentlemen," a deep voice said over the loudspeakers, "may I have your attention, please?"

Alan and Rowena broke apart to find the dance floor empty except for the two of them. They looked sheepishly at each other, and Alan wondered how long ago the band had stopped playing. He'd been too lost in their kiss to notice.

Burt Tubb stood nearby holding a microphone in one hand and an envelope in the other. "Let's give a round of applause to Rowena Dahl and Alan Rand, voted this year's Most Romantic Couple.''

Cheers and knowing smiles broke out in the crowd around them. Rowena glanced at Alan, a becoming pink blush on her cheeks. His gaze fell to her full, luscious mouth, and he wanted to kiss her all over again.

Burt handed the envelope to Alan. ''The prize is a romantic dinner for two at Tubb's Café, home of some of the best service and finest local cuisine you'll find anywhere in the state.''

The crowd laughed at Burt's blatant self-promotion.

''Thanks,'' Alan said, handing the envelope to Rowena. Her cheeks still looked flushed, but he saw the glow of pride in her eyes. At that moment, he realized what kissing him on the dance floor meant. The people of Cooper's Corner believed that he and Rowena were a couple.

She had just confirmed it for them.

An odd sensation rippled like a feather across his chest. He suddenly had an inexplicable urge to laugh. To grab Rowena in his arms and whirl her around in a circle. Clearing his throat, he wondered what the hell was coming over him. Had the dance committee put something unusual in that punch?

''Now it's time for our winners to enjoy their spotlight dance,'' Burt announced, then motioned to the band to begin playing.

The overhead lights dimmed in the gymnasium, and a moment later Alan and Rowena found themselves bathed in the glow of the spotlight. She moved toward him with a self-conscious smile as a jazzy rendition of the song "It Had To Be You" filled the air.

"Are you terribly embarrassed?" she asked, walking into his arms.

"Standing in the spotlight is a first for me," he admitted, moving to the beat of the music. "Although I was once voted most valuable player on my soccer team."

"What was the prize?"

"A black eye from the team captain. He didn't like anyone but himself to be the center of attention."

She smiled at him, her blond hair gleaming like spun gold in the glare of the spotlight. "Don't worry. I won't let anybody here lay a hand on you."

He gazed into her eyes. "There are some hands on me that I don't mind at all."

Her blush deepened, and she moved closer to rest her head on his shoulder. Her hair brushed lightly against his cheek, and he inhaled deeply, relishing her familiar scent.

"I love this song," she murmured.

"It's the perfect one for us," he replied, "if you listen to the words. Especially considering the way we met. Have you ever thought about it, Rowena?"

She pulled back far enough to look at his face. "Thought about what?"

"The way we met. What if that mistake at the Orr Fertility Clinic wasn't a mistake at all. What if it was fate?"

Her amethyst eyes widened. "Do you really believe that, Alan?"

"I don't know," he replied truthfully. "All I do

know is that this is the craziest thing that's ever happened to me. That sperm switch brought us together. And right now I can't imagine any place else I'd rather be.''

"Do you want to hear something really crazy? Neither can I.''

He closed his eyes as he rested his cheek against the top of her head. For the first time in a very long while he didn't feel alone anymore. What was it about her that intrigued him so much? He'd met countless glamorous women in his business, but none of them had had the same effect on him as Rowena. Was it because he knew she carried his child? Or was there something more? Something he'd never experienced before?

"Alan?" she asked as the band began to play the song a second time and the other couples joined them on the dance floor.

"Yes?"

She looked at him with a mischievous smile. "Did I mention I bought some bananas today? Along with a gallon of Neapolitan ice cream? I have chocolate syrup and strawberries and pineapple, too. All the makings for a banana split." Her eyes flashed with something that made his body tighten. "In case you still have that craving."

He looked into her eyes. "I definitely have a craving. But not for a banana split."

She licked her lips. "Do you think anyone will mind if the Most Romantic Couple leaves the dance early?"

"I don't care," he said, guiding her toward the

door. His heart pounded at the promise he'd just seen in her eyes. Some small voice in his head told him this was all happening too fast. He'd made it a practice to err on the side of caution where women were concerned. Made it perfectly clear that he wasn't interested in a commitment before he embarked on a relationship.

But this was different. This was Rowena. And for the first time in his life, he was letting his heart take full control.

FIFTEEN MINUTES later they were on her front porch. Neither of them had spoken during the short ride to her house. Alan's body throbbed with need, and he hoped Rowena hadn't changed her mind in the interim. He wanted her. She wanted him. Had anything in the world ever been more simple?

But by the time she unlocked the door and they walked inside, nothing seemed simple anymore. What if he moved too fast? What if he disappointed her? Wiping his damp palms on his slacks, he watched her walk to the hearth and bend to place a log on the iron grate. His body hardened in an instant.

This was ridiculous. He was as nervous as a randy teenager. Alan took a deep, calming breath as she stoked the fire. A few moments later, a blaze crackled up from the logs, and Alan got his runaway hormones under control.

Rowena turned away from the hearth to face him, the golden flames of the fire casting an ethereal glow around her. He stopped breathing for a moment as he looked at her. She was incredible, both inside and out.

She moved toward him. "Have you changed your mind about the banana split?"

He swallowed, finding it hard to think with all the blood in his body rushing south. "What?"

A smile played on her lips. "I've got plenty of whipped cream...if you're interested."

"I'm definitely interested." Alan pulled her to him, cupping her face in his hands. "But not in whipped cream. I just want you."

"Show me," she whispered.

So he did. With his mouth. His hands. His body. A few moments later, it was as if that tense drive from the dance had never happened. They were as frantic for each other as they had been on the dance floor. Together they pulled off coats and gloves and hats in their need to come closer. He stifled a groan as her hands circled his neck and she pressed her body against him.

Was it possible this gorgeous woman could want him as much as he wanted her? Alan didn't take time to question it, he just indulged in the taste and feel of her, knowing he could never get enough.

Rowena unknotted his tie, then took his hand and led him to the thick woven rug in front of the fireplace. She reached for the top button of his shirt, slipping it out of the hole with excruciating slowness, a seductive light in her eyes. She destroyed him one button at a time. His body was on fire an eternity later as she parted his shirt and pushed it off his shoulders. Her hands caressed his bare chest.

"Are you sure about this?" he asked, needing to

know now, before it was impossible for him to stop. Her touch almost made him dizzy.

"I want to make love to the father of my baby." Then she leaned forward and flicked her tongue over his flat nipple. Alan tilted his head back and closed his eyes as her mouth dropped dewy kisses over his chest.

Rowena explored his body with her hands, first pushing him down on the rug, then molding her palms against his chest and sprinkling sweet kisses over his face. When she nipped at his earlobe, her warm breath sent a tingle throughout his entire body, inflaming him even more. He pulled her on top of him, welcoming the weight of her body against his straining flesh. Blood pooled low as he captured her lips with his mouth.

His tongue swept inside her sweet mouth, pouring all the passion, all the longing that he'd stored up for a lifetime into that kiss. Going slow wasn't an option. His fingers found the zipper on the back of her dress and slid it all the way down to her waist.

When he broke the kiss, she rolled off him, then rose to her knees. Meeting his gaze, she slowly, seductively pulled the straps off her shoulders and let the dress shimmy down the length of her body, revealing the red silk bra and panties underneath. Then she unhooked the front clasp of the bra, and her generous breasts spilled out.

He knelt before her and cupped her breasts in his hands, molding and shaping them until she tipped her head back and emitted a low, wanton moan. The sound almost drove him over the edge.

His hands slid downward, over the gentle slope of her belly to the waistband of her panties. He rubbed his palms over the silky fabric, loving the way her eyes glazed at the sensation. He leaned down to kiss her again, tracing the seam of her lips with his tongue. She opened for him, and he groaned when he entered the silky haven of her mouth.

Their tongues tangled and tantalized, heightening the tension between them to a fever pitch. No longer could he indulge in a slow seduction. He wanted her with an urgency that seemed to match hers.

In the space of a heartbeat, he shed his slacks and shoes. Her gaze slid over him like warm honey, and he hoped she wasn't disappointed in what she saw.

''Oh, my,'' she breathed in appreciation, her eyes widening a fraction. Then she lay back on the rug and held her hand out to him.

He joined her there, savoring the skin to skin contact. The heat from the blaze behind him was nothing compared with the fire building inside him. She whispered what she wanted in his ear, and he made it his mission to fulfill every wish.

When he couldn't wait any longer, he sat up to drag her panties off. Then he leaned back to savor the sight of her completely naked, her perfect body basking in the firelight. She was like a fantasy come to life, and he hoped like hell he wasn't dreaming.

She held out her arms to him, her long blond hair splayed over the rug. Hovering above her on his elbows, he let the moment linger between them.

But he couldn't wait long. He had to kiss her. To touch her. To be so close to her he couldn't tell where he ended and she began. He'd never desired that kind of intimacy before and it rattled him a little, but he was too caught up in the passion between them to care. He bent to worship the nipple of one breast, swirling his tongue around it until it formed an erect peak. He closed his lips over it, sucking gently, and her fingers plucked at his hair, her head thrown back.

He moved to the other breast, giving it the same undivided attention. His hand moved lower, sliding over her body in a way that drew a delicious moan from deep in her throat.

At last she looked into his face, her lips parted. ''I love you,'' she breathed, then gasped aloud when his fingers touched just the right spot. ''Oh, Alan. Now. Please.''

He didn't wait for a second invitation. Sheathing himself inside her, he groaned with satisfaction as she wrapped her long legs around him. His lone conscious thought was not to put too much weight on her stomach. Holding her tightly in his arms, he turned so that both of them lay on their sides.

''You're incredible,'' he rasped, unable to keep from moving inside her. He wanted to savor this moment. The feel of her around him. The sparks of desire in her eyes. The soft press of her breasts against him. But he couldn't think about anything when she writhed her hips to bring him even farther inside her.

Her eyelids fluttered closed as they moved together in a timeless rhythm. He watched her, cradling her face in his hands, loving the play of expressions on her beautiful face.

When her breathing quickened, he shifted slightly

and saw her gasp with pleasure as she reached out to
cling to him. When he heard her cry out his name, he
pulled her on top of him and triggered a second climax
deep within her moments later. Then he released his
last thread of control, losing himself inside her.

And finding a love he didn't know existed.

ROWENA LAY sheltered in Alan's arms as the fire cast
a golden glow over their naked bodies. His lips nuz-
zled her hair, and she closed her eyes, trying to pre-
serve this perfect moment in her memory.

She feared this tranquil peace between them
couldn't last. They'd still made no decisions about the
baby. Was this the lull before the coming storm? But
instead of battening down her heart to minimize the
damage, she let her love for him flow through her with
the full force of a gale.

"So tell me the truth," he murmured in her ear.
"Am I better than Sloane?"

She laughed as she turned in his arms to face him.
"I think you've been watching too many of those *Another Dawn* videotapes."

"Too many of him kissing you, anyway," Alan
bent his head to brush his lips over her brow. "I sus-
pect the guy threw in a few extra kisses that weren't
in the script, didn't he?"

"Of course not. He was a professional." Her eyes
widened as she looked at him. "Are you actually jealous of a character on a soap opera?"

He scowled. "Hell, no. I just hate his guts."

She smiled as she snuggled closer to him. "If you

were a true fan of the show, you'd know my heart really belongs to Derrick.''

"Not anymore," he said huskily, tightening his arms around her.

"No," she breathed, "not anymore." It was time she finally faced the truth. She loved Alan Rand. Loved him more than she ever thought it was possible to love a man. Now she knew why she'd waited thirty-six years to let someone into her life. She'd been waiting for this. Waiting for him.

"Now answer me another question," he said, his hand trailing over her hip.

"Anything," she said, her body softening under his tender touch.

He reached up to cradle her cheek, turning her face to him. "Will you marry me, Rowena?"

Thunder rumbled in her soul as she looked into his warm brown eyes. "I...don't know what to say."

"Say yes," he entreated, a smile tipping up one corner of his mouth. "It's the perfect solution to our problem. The perfect gift for our baby."

The perfect solution. Despite the heat from the fire, a chill swept through her. Was she a problem he'd been unable to solve until now? Did love for her even enter into his equation? But that wasn't fair. She'd considered him a problem, too. One that seemed to get bigger with each passing day. One that now seemed gargantuan after what had just taken place between them.

"You're making me nervous," he said, tilting her chin with his finger. "Just for your information, I've never proposed to a woman before. But I don't think it's supposed to take this long for her to answer."

She licked her dry lips. "This is so...sudden. We've only known each other a few weeks."

He brushed his thumb over her lower lip, sending a tingle straight down to her toes. "I already know I want to spend the rest of my life with the two of you."

The two of you. Despite what he'd said about fate earlier this evening, she couldn't help but wonder if he was only with her because of the baby. How could she possibly accept his marriage proposal without knowing for sure? But she couldn't reject it, either. Not when her heart yearned for a future she'd only dared dream about. A future with the man she loved.

"May I have some time to think about it?" She hedged, hating herself for wimping out. But she couldn't bring herself to destroy this sweet intimacy between them.

He leaned over to kiss the tip of her nose. "Of course you can have some time. I'm not going anywhere." Then a crease furrowed his brow as he studied her expression. "Is something wrong, Rowena?"

She nestled closer to him so he couldn't see her face. "So much has happened lately. I just don't want to rush into anything."

His body relaxed against her. "You're right. The last thing I want to do is add more stress to your life."

Too late.

Rowena closed her eyes, wishing she knew the right thing to do. There were no soap opera writers around to pen a happy ending to this story.

She had to figure it out by herself.

CHAPTER SIXTEEN

ROWENA found herself alone in the house the next afternoon. She and Alan had made love again in the early morning hours. The passion between them had been so intense, she'd almost flung her concerns aside and said yes. *Almost.* What had held her back? Fear? Common sense? Lingering doubts about the man she loved?

That man had been hit with a sudden inspiration to make a cradle today. He'd taken off a couple of hours ago for the hardware store in New Ashford. Since he'd just been complaining about all the work piling up in his briefcase, she thought it sounded more like procrastination than inspiration. Especially since Alan had sheepishly admitted to her that he didn't have any carpentry experience.

But it touched her all the same. She might question his feelings for her, but his love for the baby was obvious. He'd make a wonderful father. She just wished that was a good enough reason to marry him. After watching her parents' marriage fall apart, Rowena knew that nothing but the strongest love could lead her to that kind of commitment. The risk was too great.

Rowena walked into the kitchen and filled the teapot with water before setting it on the stove. The granite counters and stainless steel appliances gleamed. She was amazed at how immaculate and organized Alan had kept her home while she was confined to her bed. Even more amazing was that he seemed to enjoy it.

As she leaned against the counter, waiting for the water to boil, her thoughts drifted to last night. No man had ever touched her that way before. Just remembering the things his hands did to her sent a delicious shiver through her body.

But were they moving too fast? He'd only arrived in Cooper's Corner a few weeks ago. She'd waited thirty-six years to find Mr. Right. How could she be certain Alan was that man, just because he was kind and handsome and caring and sexy? An aspiring cook and housekeeper who not only picked up after himself, but her, too. A fantastic lover. Rowena smiled as the teapot began to whistle. Most women would kill for a man like that. So what exactly was she waiting for?

Love.

One simple word. When Alan proposed to her last night, he hadn't mentioned one word about love. Worse, he'd told her that marriage was the best solution to their problem.

She'd given him her heart as well as her body last night. Even told him she loved him. But he'd never said a word about her declaration. At the time, she'd been too caught up in the moment to notice. But now his silence on the subject seemed deafening.

The telephone rang, breaking her reverie. She reached across the counter for the receiver. "Hello?"

"Is this Rowena Dahl?" asked a cheery masculine voice on the other end of the line.

"Yes." She retrieved a tin of hot chocolate from the cupboard.

"Hello, there! This is Daryl Tubb."

It took her a moment to place him. Daryl Tubb. Burt and Lori's son. A real estate agent from Williamstown who always came on a little too strong— especially to young, single women. She'd only spoken to him once or twice in her life. So why was he calling? "Hello, Daryl."

"How is everything in Cooper's Corner?"

"Same as always." She poured hot water from the teapot into her favorite ceramic mug. "Is there something I can do for you?"

"As a matter of fact," he replied, "I've got a couple of prospective buyers who might be interested in your shop. They're looking for a good property to open an antique store. So if you can tell me what you're asking—"

"Wait a minute," Rowena interjected. "What makes you think my shop is for sale?"

"My dad mentioned something about it when I called home last weekend. Said he heard it from the guy you're living with—that you're planning to move to Canada."

Her hand tightened around the receiver. "Alan told your father my barbershop is for sale?"

"Why else would I be calling?" Daryl asked. "Now, look, I'm sure we can negotiate a selling price that will make everybody happy. I can bring my clients down for a walk-through at your convenience.

They're eager to get their business started, Rowena. This could be a great opportunity for you."

"Hold it, Daryl," she said, still trying to comprehend what was happening. "I'm not interested in selling."

"I can get you top price," he persisted.

"Cooper's Corner is my home," she replied, frustrated with Alan for putting her in this position. And with interfering in her life. "I'm not planning to go anywhere."

Had Alan told the whole town he was moving her to Toronto? Without bothering to mention it to her? Maybe that's why so few of her customers had called to make appointments now that she was back on her feet. Were they already looking for another barber?

Daryl sighed. "Well, if you change your mind, you know who to call."

"Thank you," she said blankly, then hung up the telephone. Perhaps she was overreacting. No matter how it sounded, she shouldn't automatically assume the worst. She knew how easily rumors grew in Cooper's Corner. There was no proof that Alan had tried to sell her barbershop. No proof that he was trying to control her life.

But her fingers still shook as she pried the lid off the tin of hot chocolate. She turned and pulled open the silverware drawer to retrieve a spoon.

That's when she saw it.

A small wedge of powder blue paper sticking out from underneath the molded silverware tray. She lifted it and pulled out an envelope addressed to Savannah Corrington. Something cold and heavy settled in Rowena's stomach as she looked at it. The seal was unbroken, but it was postmarked over a week ago. She slit open the envelope and pulled out the letter inside. It was written in the same creepy style as before.

Dear Savannah,

You know how much I adore you, yet you continue to ignore me. I won't stand for it. You belong to me. We are meant to be together. What must I do to convince you we are soul mates? How much more must I suffer?

Do you ever think of me? Ever mourn our love? I count the days and the hours until we can be together again. Don't make me wait too long, my darling. Don't make me sorry I gave you my heart.

All my love, Sloane

She dropped the letter on the counter, feeling sick inside. After all these years, why had Max Heller suddenly come back into her life? Rowena stuffed the letter into the envelope, knowing she didn't have any choice. She'd have to go to the police.

The front door opened, and Alan called, "Wait until you see the great pattern I found for the cradle. It looks a little complicated, but I've got almost five months to figure it out."

She walked into the living room and saw him stomping snow off his boots, his arms full of lumber.

"I'm freezing," he said, smiling at her. "Are you interested in warming me up?" Then he saw the expression on her face, and his smile faded. "What's wrong?"

"I found the letter."

His brow furrowed. "What letter?" The confusion in his eyes cleared when he realized what she meant. "Oh, right. The one from your old boyfriend."

She didn't know which surprised her more. The fact that he so openly admitted to hiding the letter. Or that he knew Max had sent it. But how? "The letter wasn't opened. How do you know it's from Max?"

"Because it was addressed to Savannah Corrington on a powder blue envelope." He set the lumber on the rug, then brushed off his hands "I know about the letter he sent you before, Rowena. I overheard Maureen talking about it on the phone."

Rowena couldn't believe her friend would break a confidence. Then she remembered Maureen admitting she'd contacted a cop she knew in New York to look into the matter. But that was almost three weeks ago. Alan hadn't said a word about it. "When exactly did you overhear that conversation?"

He shrugged out of his coat. "The night you came over to Twin Oaks and proposed a truce between us."

Her stomach tensed. "I don't believe this."

He moved to her side, his face etched with concern. "I think you'd better sit down. You look pale."

She didn't move. She was through with men telling her what to do. "You've known about that letter from Max all this time?"

"Yes," Alan admitted. "Frankly, I've been pretty concerned. It sounds like the guy is unstable."

"So why didn't you say anything about it that night?"

He folded his arms across his broad chest. "If you remember, we hadn't been on the best of terms. So I thought it would be better to just agree to your truce so I could keep an eye on you."

"Keep an eye on me?" she echoed.

"In case Heller tried anything. I heard Maureen say you didn't want to contact the police. Someone had to look out for you and the baby."

She gave a slow nod. "So that's why you so readily accepted my dinner invitation."

"Don't make it sound so calculating." He took a step toward her. "Sure, I wanted to protect you from Heller, but it was more than that."

She met his gaze, trying to stay calm. Did he have other secrets he was keeping from her? Other plans for the future that he hadn't deigned to tell her? "What else?"

He turned toward the fire. "I don't know. A chance to get to know you better, I guess. Hell, you're the mother of my baby. Don't you think that's a good enough reason?"

It should be. But for some reason it didn't satisfy her. She'd proposed a truce between them to see if Alan was really serious about taking on the responsibilities of becoming a father. But she hadn't planned to fall in love with him along the way. Everything was more complicated than ever.

He turned to face her. "I don't understand why you're so upset about this. So I hid the stupid letter. I still think I did the right thing."

Her jaw tightened. "That's the problem."

He blinked. "What do you mean? I was trying to protect you."

"I'm thirty-six years old, Alan. I don't need anyone to protect me."

A muscle flexed in his jaw. "You've had enough stress in your life lately. I wasn't about to let this Max Heller cause even more."

"But who gave you the right to start making unilateral decisions about *my* life?"

His eyes narrowed. "You don't trust me?"

"That's not the point." She shook her head, sadness tightening her throat. He didn't even begin to understand. "I left Max because he thought he always knew what was best for me. It started with little things. Like screening my telephone calls and picking out clothes for me to wear. Then it got progressively worse, until he wanted to imprison me in a cocoon and never let me go."

"I'm glad you got away from him," Alan replied. "He sounds like a complete jerk."

She swallowed hard. "But you're doing the same thing."

He recoiled as if she'd struck him. "You're comparing me to Heller?"

"You hid the letter," she said by way of an example. "And you're telling people that my barbershop is for sale. I just got a call from a real estate agent!"

"Wait a minute," Alan replied, his voice rising. "All I did was stop in at Tubb's Café for coffee one morning and got into a discussion about land prices around here. I simply asked about the current market for a place as nice as your shop. Is that so terrible?''

She glared at him, completely exasperated. "When did I *ever* tell you I was selling it?''

"We talked about your moving to Toronto." He began pacing back and forth across the same rug they'd made love on the night before. "I guess I just assumed the rest. I wanted you to get a good price. I *thought* I was doing you a favor.''

"Max always thought the same way.''

He whirled on her, furious sparks in his eyes. "Stop comparing me to him! I'm not out to hurt you.''

"I know,'' she admitted, then squared her shoulders. "But you want to control me. In the end, it's the same thing.''

"Control you?'' He stared at her in stunned disbelief. "I asked you to marry me. I want you to be my wife.''

"Why?'' she asked, though she wasn't certain she wanted to hear the answer.

"Why do you think?'' he replied, his voice laced with anger and confusion. "So we can be a family.''

She closed her eyes. "That's what I thought.''

He moved toward her. "Look, Rowena, I'm sorry if you're upset about the letter. Maybe I should have showed it to you right away. But you'd just come home from the hospital, and I wasn't about to take any chances with the baby.''

She nodded, sympathizing with his fear for the baby. Too bad he was totally clueless about her fears. Alan simply didn't understand that she couldn't give up her independence. Not after her experience with Max.

As much as she loved Alan, she wasn't a bonus prize he could claim along with the baby. She wanted to be loved for herself. To be trusted to make her own decisions.

And she needed to accept the fact that he might never understand.

She took a deep, shuddering breath. "I think you should go back to Toronto."

His jaw sagged. "What are you talking about? I want to marry you!"

"You want the baby."

He backed away from her. "You really believe that's the only reason I proposed to you?"

She stared at her clenched fingers. "I'm not sure what to believe anymore. That's the problem. I can't take the chance of making a mistake! Not when the baby would be the one to suffer the most."

"What do you want from me?" he cried.

"I don't know," she replied, feeling sick inside. "If you had just once told me you loved me—that would have been enough."

"Damn it, Rowena! I do love you." His nostrils flared. "There. I said it."

Tears stung her eyes. "Alan, don't do this."

"Why are you doing this to us? I do love you, Rowena. Whether you want to believe it now or not. And yes, I love our baby. I want to be a father. Is that so damn much to ask?"

She placed her hand on her stomach as if to protect the baby from the harsh words ricocheting between them. "No. You'll be a good father. I want you to be part of the baby's life. I'll call my lawyer in the morning and—"

"Don't bother." He bit the words out, turning his back on her and heading down the hallway. "Since I'm such a controlling monster, I'll just handle everything myself."

She stood up. "Alan, wait…"

But he didn't turn around. A few heartbeats later he was in the living room, his suitcase in his hand. He grabbed his coat, then turned at the front door, unable to hide the despair in his eyes.

"I never thought I'd find a woman I could love with my whole heart," he said, his voice gruff. "With my soul. Maybe I don't always say the right thing at just the right moment. I'm no damn poet. But I guess you're right. We shouldn't get married. Because you don't know me at all."

Then he was gone.

Rowena stood frozen for a moment as she stared at the door. Panic assailed her when she realized he was really leaving. For good. She ran after him, but he was already in the car by the time she reached the front step.

"Alan," she called, frantically waving her arm in the air.

But he peeled away from the curb and drove into the sunset, not once looking back. The baby fluttered inside her, and Rowena placed her hands over it, the tears freezing on her cheeks.

"What have I done?"

CHAPTER SEVENTEEN

DARKNESS CLOAKED the village of Cooper's Corner when Alan finally turned his car in the direction of Twin Oaks. He'd been driving aimlessly for hours, stoking the red-hot ember of anger burning inside him. Because if he let it cool, the raw pain underneath would be unbearable.

Rowena didn't want to marry him. His hands tightened on the steering wheel as her words echoed in his brain. *If you had just once told me you loved me.*

The irony almost made him laugh out loud, but his throat constricted instead. Hadn't his father's inability to express his love been one of the main reasons Alan had come to Cooper's Corner? He was so certain he was different. He'd wanted to be a good father. To show unconditional love and support for his child. But how could he do that when the woman he loved didn't even know it?

He slowed the car when the Twin Oaks Bed and Breakfast came into view. If the Coopers didn't have a room available for him tonight, he'd have to drive to New Ashford or Williamstown. Why hadn't he headed home? If he'd been thinking straight, he would have driven directly to Toronto and consulted with Brad.

But neither his mind nor his heart was quite ready to accept the inevitable.

He grabbed his suitcase out of the back seat, then walked to the front door. It opened into the large gathering room, empty and dim except for the glow of the dying embers in the hearth.

Maureen looked at him in surprise as she descended the staircase. "Hello, Alan. I'm surprised to see you here so late." Then her gaze fell on the suitcase in his hand.

"Do you have a room available, Maureen?"

She studied him for a moment, then started down the rest of the stairs. "As a matter of fact, your same room is open. There was a couple from Rhode Island due in this afternoon, but they had to cancel their reservation at the last minute."

"I guess it's my lucky day," he said wryly, then pulled out his wallet to retrieve his credit card. "I'll just need it for one night."

"How is Rowena?" she asked, concern etched on her forehead.

"Fine." He scribbled his name in the guest ledger.

Maureen tilted her head, watching him. "*You* don't look so fine."

He tossed down the pen. "I will be. I've been through worse." Only he wasn't sure that was true. At least with the cancer, he'd had something to fight against. But this sickness was in his heart, and he didn't know how to vanquish it. He missed Rowena already. Her smile. Her laughter. Her eyes. When they'd made love last night, something inside him had felt complete. Now that old emptiness was back, and he feared it would never be gone again.

"I know it's none of my business," Maureen said softly. "But Rowena is a good friend of mine. If there is anything I can do to help…"

"It's too late," Alan blurted. He hadn't planned to talk to anyone about this except his lawyer. And maybe the nearest bartender. But the words spilled out anyway. "It's over between us. Rowena made her feelings about me perfectly clear."

Maureen arched a winged brow. "I thought her feelings about you seemed pretty clear at the Sweetheart Dance."

He raked his fingers through his hair, trying desperately to hold on to his anger. "We both know she's a good actress."

Maureen started to say something, then pressed her lips firmly together.

Alan knew he'd probably irritated her with that remark, but he couldn't get into this now. Not with his head pounding and his heart breaking. Maureen would probably learn all the details soon enough. He'd discovered in a very short time that you couldn't keep secrets in Cooper's Corner.

"Just do me one favor," he said, picking up his suitcase.

"If I can," she replied evenly.

"Rowena got another one of those letters." He shifted his suitcase from one hand to the other. "From Max Heller. Make sure she goes to the police this time. Even if you have to drag her there…." His voice trailed as he realized this was exactly the reason she'd shut him out of her life—because he thought he knew what was best for her. "I just want her to be safe."

"So do I," Maureen said. "Safe and happy."

Alan nodded, knowing he couldn't do anything about the latter—except stay out of her life.

A child's soft cry echoed down the hallway.

"Please excuse me," Maureen said. "It sounds as if one of the girls is having a nightmare."

He watched her walk away, then turned toward the staircase.

"Alan?"

He froze, the voice rolling over him like an echo from the past. He slowly turned and found himself looking at the last person he expected to see.

His father.

Alan stared at him until George Rand stepped forward. "Is this a bad time?"

He couldn't have picked a worse one. But Alan still had trouble believing the man was here at all. "I suppose it's as good as any."

George waved toward the gathering room. "Do you mind if we sit down to talk?"

Talk. After thirty-four years, Alan couldn't remember more than a handful of times when he and his father had actually talked. "Sure."

He watched his father walk to the sofa, noting how much older he looked. His hair was thinner and completely gray. He had a hitch to his step, as if arthritis had settled into one of his knees. His body was much heavier, too, with fleshiness in his cheek and jowl. It had been so long since he'd seen the man. Almost five long years. Alan couldn't be sure he would have recognized him if he'd passed him on the street.

"I found the Twin Oaks business card you left in my door," George said as he seated himself on the sofa.

Alan grabbed the wing chair across from him. "Almost three weeks ago."

"I suppose you're wondering what I'm doing here now." George shifted on the cushion as if he couldn't quite get comfortable.

That makes two of us.

"Yes." Alan wasn't in the mood to mince words tonight.

George let his gaze wander to the stone hearth, then back. He cleared his throat. "I wanted to know if you're all right, Alan. I thought maybe you came here because the cancer had spread...."

"You couldn't even bother to visit me during my treatments." Alan bit the words out. "Why would I drive seven long hours to tell you anything when it's so obvious you don't give a damn?"

"That's not true," George countered, a mottled flush in his cheeks.

Alan shook his head. "Actions speak louder than words, Dad. Not that you ever wasted many words on me." He rose to his feet, barely able to remain civil. "Look, if you came here tonight to find out if I'm dying, the answer is no. The treatments eradicated the cancer, and I have a full life ahead of me. A life I've gotten used to living without you in it. So you can just go back to pretending I don't exist."

He turned and took three long strides toward the staircase before his father's voice stopped him cold.

"I did it for you, son."

Alan whirled on him. "What the hell does that mean?"

George struggled to find the words. "It means...I wanted to protect you. Or maybe I was just too damn proud to let my son find out I was a drunk."

He walked slowly toward his father. "I don't know what you're talking about."

George met his gaze. "That's because I knew how to hide it. Most nights, I'd come home from the bar so drunk I could barely stand up straight. Then I'd hide behind a newspaper and try to keep from passing out."

Alan tried to comprehend what his father was telling him, but he kept remembering snatches of their past. How George Rand would retire to bed at a ridiculously early hour, usually long before ten o'clock. How he always carried a supply of peppermints in his pocket. Had he used them to cover the odor of booze on his breath?

"I was a closet drunk, Alan," George admitted. "I could put in a full day's work without any problem, but as soon as I punched out my time card for the day, I'd hit the bar. Then I'd drive home in a haze and not remember much of anything until the next day."

"But surely Mom knew."

George nodded. "I'm sure she did. But she never said anything. Or even asked me to stop. I think that was part of the problem."

Alan clenched his hands into fists. "You're blaming her for the fact that you were a drunk?"

"No," George said hastily. "She was a wonderful woman. I think she truly believed she was helping me by not nagging about my drinking." He got a faraway look in his faded brown eyes. "But sometimes I wonder what would have happened if she'd confronted me about it. Or even threatened to leave me. But that never happened, so I simply didn't have a reason to stop."

"Except for me," Alan said bitterly, realizing his father had preferred spending his free time with a bottle rather than his own son.

George nodded, his voice growing thick. "When I found out you had Hodgkin's disease, I finally realized how much time I had wasted." He slowly shook his head. "That I might lose you before I got a chance to know you."

"Did you really care?"

"Hell, yes, I cared," George exclaimed. "For the first time in over thirty years, I cared about something more than losing myself in a bottle."

Alan sank into the chair again. "So why didn't you ever try to quit?"

"I did." His mouth curved with a humorless smile. "Three times in the last three years. I swore to myself I'd get sober so I could help you through the treatments. The first time I lasted four weeks. The next time I made it for eleven whole months."

"And the third time?" Alan asked.

"I've been clean and sober for almost two years. But I still want a drink every single day." He looked at his hands. "I'm not sure I can make it, Alan. That's why I never came to see you during your treatments. And why I almost didn't come here tonight. I can't stand the thought of letting you down." He sucked in a deep breath. "I'm a weak man, Alan. And I've always believed a father should be strong for his son."

"I didn't need you to be strong." Alan's throat contracted. "I just needed you to be there for me. If you had just told me you loved me—that would have been enough."

George looked at him. "I love you, son. I always have."

Tears stung his eyes, and Alan realized how much it meant to hear the words spoken from the heart. Not flung out in anger, the way he'd said them to Rowena a short while ago.

Alan half rose from his chair to hug his father, but something held him back. Maybe all those years of distance between them. He really didn't know his father at all. But for the first time, he believed that someday he would. And when that day came, a hug would be as natural as breathing.

"So if you didn't come to Cooper's Corner to see me," George said, rapidly blinking back the tears gleaming in his eyes, "why are you here?"

He swallowed a sigh. "It's a long story, Dad."

"I'd like to hear it," George said evenly. "But only if you want to tell me."

Alan hesitated, then leaned back in his chair. "Well, there's this girl...."

ON MONDAY MORNING, Rowena found herself jumping up every time the telephone rang. But instead of

Alan, it was always one of her customers ready to fill her schedule once again. So much for her fears that Alan's inquiries about selling her shop had driven customers away. Most of them told her they'd wanted to wait to make an appointment to be certain she was fully recovered from her ordeal.

When the doorbell rang shortly after ten o'clock, her heart leaped in her chest. She hurried toward the door, telling herself not to get her hopes up. After the way she'd treated Alan on Saturday, he'd probably never come back.

Maureen stood on the other side of the door. She took one look at Rowena's face and frowned. "Is something wrong?"

"No." Rowena forced a smile. "I'm fine." She didn't want to burden her friend any more. This was one problem she had to handle on her own. "It's nice to see you. Come on in."

"I can't stay long," Maureen told her, wiping her boots on the floor mat. "But I wanted to stop by because I finally have some news about Max Heller."

Rowena took her coat. "Good news, I hope."

"Unexpected news, anyway," Maureen replied, then turned to face her. "He passed away a month ago, Rowena."

She blinked in surprise. "But the letters…"

"Why don't you sit down," Maureen suggested, "and I'll tell you everything."

Rowena walked to the sofa, her mind spinning. This didn't make sense. If Max was dead, who had sent those letters? And why?

"Are you sure you're feeling all right?" Maureen asked. "How is the baby?"

"We're both fine," Rowena assured her, even though it wasn't exactly true. She hadn't been fine since Alan walked out the door. The problem was, she didn't know how to get him back. Or if she should try. She kept waffling back and forth. Missing him terribly one moment and telling herself it was for the best the next.

Rowena settled back against the sofa. "Now tell me about Max."

Maureen grew solemn. "He died of a drug overdose, Rowena. Apparently, he's had a heavy cocaine and methamphetamine habit for several years."

Rowena frowned in confusion. "He never touched drugs when I knew him. But if he's dead, where did those letters come from?"

"My friend at the NYPD traced them to Max's mother." Maureen leaned forward. "She was devastated by his sudden death, Rowena. When the police confronted her about the letters, she broke down and told them Max began using drugs shortly after you broke up with him. She blamed you when his life started falling apart. After his funeral, she began sorting through his personal belongings and found letters he'd never sent to you."

"But how did she know where to find me?"

"Mrs. Heller contacted the producer of *Another Dawn* on the pretext of notifying you about Max's death. Her plan was to send you one letter a week. I still don't quite understand why."

"To make me pay for hurting her son," Rowena breathed.

"Are you all right?" Maureen asked softly.

She nodded. "I will be. In fact, part of me understands Mrs. Heller. She loved her son so much, despite his flaws. That's how a mother is supposed to feel, isn't it?"

"Not if it ultimately hurts someone else," Maureen replied. "Mrs. Heller wouldn't allow herself to see the fact that her son had serious problems, so instead she blamed you for his death."

"I still feel sorry for her."

"I know." Maureen folded her hands together in her lap. "Mrs. Heller isn't going to bother you anymore, Rowena. She turned over the rest of the unsent letters to the police and agreed to see a grief counselor."

"I hope she gets the help she needs," Rowena murmured. "Thank you for coming here and telling me about Max."

"You're welcome." Maureen stood to take her leave. "There's something else. I wasn't sure if I should say anything, but I thought you might want to know."

Rowena rose to her feet. "What?"

"Alan Rand checked out of Twin Oaks early yesterday morning and headed for Toronto."

Despair settled into the pit of her stomach. "He did?"

Maureen nodded. "He definitely wasn't himself, Rowena. I take it something happened between the two of you?"

Rowena bit her lip to keep it from quivering. "He asked me to marry him."

"And you turned him down?" Maureen ventured.

She nodded. "Only now I'm not quite sure why. I found a letter from Max, or rather his mother, in the kitchen drawer. Alan hid it from me while I was confined to bed. He told me he did it to shield me from more stress."

Maureen slowly nodded. "I might have done the same thing under the circumstances."

That didn't make her feel any better. "He was also asking around town about the fair market price for my barbershop."

Maureen frowned. "You're moving?"

"No." Rowena turned and walked to the window, staring out at the snowy brightness. "We talked about my living in Toronto after the baby was born, but nothing was ever settled. So when I found the letter and got the telephone call, it upset me. I accused him of trying to control my life."

"Like Max," Maureen said.

"No." Rowena turned to face her. "Alan is nothing like Max. He tried to tell me that, but I wouldn't listen. Max wanted power over me. If I defied him, he'd try to find some way to hurt or humiliate me—all in the name of love. Max told me a hundred times over how much he loved me." She tried to laugh, but it came out as a sob. "That's what's so ridiculous."

"I don't understand."

"I told Alan I couldn't marry him because he never said the words *I love you*. Words Max had said constantly, but never really meant."

Rowena closed her eyes, remembering the pain she'd seen in Alan's eyes. "I never should have compared him to Max. It was so unfair. I know in my heart that everything that Alan did, he did because he cares about me. About my happiness. Two men could never be more different."

Maureen moved to her. "So tell Alan how you really feel."

Rowena shook her head. "I'm afraid it's too late."

"Last time I checked, love didn't have an expiration date." Maureen reached for Rowena's hands, clasping them in hers. "If you lose Alan because of what happened in your past, then you're still allowing Max to control you."

Rowena blinked at her friend as the truth of her words sunk in. "You're right." Hope glimmered like a faraway star. "But how can I ever be certain Alan wants me for me alone?" she asked. "Not just because of the baby?"

"I don't know the answer to that," Maureen replied. "You may never find out. So you have to decide if Alan is worth the risk."

CHAPTER EIGHTEEN

TWO DAYS LATER, Rowena opened the front door to retrieve her newspaper off the stoop. A creaking sound made her turn, and she saw Alan sitting on her porch swing. Her heart skipped a beat, and a dozen emotions skittered through her as she met his enigmatic gaze.

"Hello," he said, rising from the swing, his ears red from the cold.

He sounded cordial enough, but she could feel the tension coiled between them. Remembered the hurtful words they'd exchanged. She pulled her robe more tightly around her, not certain she could stand to hear his voice raised in anger again. Or bear to see the raw pain in his eyes.

"What are you doing here?" she asked at last. "I thought you went back to Toronto."

"I did." He rose from the swing. "But I came back because I think we need to talk."

"It's only seven o'clock in the morning." She couldn't help staring at him. Feasting her gaze on his handsome face. He'd only been gone for four days, but it had seemed like an eternity.

Especially when she'd kept replaying their break up over and over in her mind, wincing at some of the things she'd said.

"I can come back later if you want."

"If it's about the baby," she began, her body trembling, but not from the cold, "I've already talked to my lawyer and told him I want us to share joint custody. I think my baby will be lucky to have you as a father, Alan."

"I hope so."

An awkward silence settled between them. Rowena had to force herself not to reach out and smooth his rumpled hair. She had no right to touch him anymore.

Then Alan's gaze skimmed from her face to her slippered feet. "You look cold."

"Why are you here?" she asked, unable to stand the suspense any longer.

"To keep a promise." He held out a small lavender gift bag, the top secured by an iridescent white ribbon.

She hesitated, then took it from him, almost afraid to open it. "I don't understand."

"Go ahead and open it," he prodded, stuffing his bare hands in his coat pockets, "and I think you will."

She hesitated, then took it from him, staring at the shiny ribbon adorning the gift bag. Rowena had never considered herself a coward, but she was suddenly terrified. Was this some kind of peace offering? She loved him so much. But could she let him back into her life when doubts still lingered? If it didn't work out between them, she knew it could completely destroy her.

"I am not leaving here, Rowena Dahl," Alan vowed, obviously sensing her apprehension, "until you open that bag and see what's inside."

Rowena knew he was just stubborn enough to do

it. They'd both die of hypothermia if she delayed any longer. Steeling herself against the tidal wave of uncertainty that threatened to engulf her, she tore off the ribbon and opened the bag.

"What is this all about, Alan?" she asked, slowly lifting her head to look at him.

"It's about keeping a promise."

Taking a deep breath, she pulled out a stuffed purple giraffe. "I thought they'd sold the last one at the store."

"They did."

"Then where did you find this one?"

"San Francisco."

She blinked at him in surprise. "How?"

A nervous smile tipped up the corner of his mouth. For a moment he looked more like a boy than a formidable man. "I asked Philo Cooper for the name of the distributor for that brand of stuffed animals. Then I called that guy, who told me he was sold out of them. But he gave me the name of the company that produced the giraffes. They faxed me a list of stores that carried their products." He gave a small shrug. "I just called around until I found one."

He made it sound so simple, but she knew it must have taken him hours to track it down. "I can't believe it."

"See," he said, one corner of his mouth twitching, "some of us controlling types can use our powers for good. I started looking for another giraffe the day after you were released from the hospital. I would have told you, but I wanted it to be a surprise."

She clutched the giraffe to her chest, feeling a ridiculous urge to cry. "I don't know how to thank you."

"I do." He moved closer to her. "Give me another chance. I love you, Rowena."

Part of her feared this was all a fantastic dream. Feared she'd wake up to face the same emptiness that had engulfed her when he'd walked out the door last Saturday.

His gaze softened as it caressed her face. "And I want to prove it to you."

Rowena swallowed, her throat tight. She'd accused Max of wanting to wrap her in a cocoon and protect her from the world. But wasn't she doing the same thing to herself? Alan Rand loved her. Not just with words, but with deeds. Clearing the icy patch off her sidewalk. Holding her and encouraging her when she went into premature labor. Feeding her tapioca pudding. Drawing her a bath. Tracking down a stuffed giraffe at the opposite end of the country.

"You don't have to prove it to me, Alan. You already have—in a million different ways." Her breath came out in little puffs of frosty air. "I'm so sorry, Alan. I never should have compared you to Max. You are nothing like him."

He moved another step closer to her. "I've missed you."

"I've missed you, too," she whispered, her heart beating double time in her chest. The fear inside her evolved into apprehension that she'd say or do the wrong thing, and shatter this fragile harmony between them. But the compassion she saw in his brown eyes gave her a glimmer of hope.

"I never want you to wonder if I only proposed to you because of the baby."

"Alan," she interjected, but he held up a hand to forestall her.

He knew this was his one chance. If he blew it now, he might never get another. He hadn't slept for the last three nights, worried he was about to make a mistake he'd regret forever. But at this moment, he knew down deep in his very soul that it was the right thing to do. "I have something else for you."

He pulled a legal envelope out of his pocket and handed it to her.

"What is this?"

He sucked in a deep breath of cold air. "A reason you can trust me."

She opened the envelope and pulled out the piece of paper he'd asked Brad to prepare for him. His friend had argued with him endlessly and almost refused to do it. But Alan had insisted.

Small snowdrifts filled the corners of the porch, and icicles hung from the eaves of the roof. He'd counted every one of them this morning while the sun had come up and he'd waited for her to appear. It had kept him from ceaseless worrying about how she'd react when she saw him on her swing.

She flipped through the sheaf of papers in her hand, and her gaze skipped rapidly over the lengthy paragraphs. "I'm not sure I understand."

"It's a legal document, signed and notarized. I'm surrendering my rights to the baby."

She stared at him. "But, Alan…"

"I love you, Rowena," he interjected before she

could continue. "But even more, I trust you to make the right decision for our baby." He cleared his throat. "I won't say it was easy for me. In fact, it was one of the hardest things I've ever had to do."

"Then why did you?" she breathed.

"Because I know one thing for certain," he said huskily. "No matter what happens, our child will be much better off if we're friends instead of enemies."

Tears flooded her amethyst eyes. "I want to be more than friends, Alan. I want to be your lover. And more than anything, I want to be your wife."

His heart leaped. "Then you'll marry me?"

"Yes." She smiled as the tears spilled from her eyes. "Any day you want."

He pulled her into his arms, holding her tight and saying a silent prayer of thanks. Then he kissed her, trying to convey the depth of his love and passion.

At last, he lifted his head to see the tears on her rosy cheeks sparkling with tiny ice crystals from the cold. Circling his arm around her waist, he turned them both toward the door. "Let's go inside where it's warm."

"Wait a minute," she replied, holding back. "I have a present for you, too."

His arm dropped away as he looked at her in surprise. "You do?"

She nodded, then took the notarized release he'd just given her and ripped it in two. He watched in astonishment as she tore it again and again, until the tiny shreds of paper were dotting the concrete porch like giant snowflakes.

Alan couldn't believe his eyes. "Rowena, what are you doing?"

"Showing you how much I trust you." She moved into his arms. "But there's more."

He wasn't certain his heart could take much more. It was so full he was afraid it might burst. Watching her tear up that release had touched something inside his soul. He knew beyond any doubt that he'd done the right thing.

She took his hand and pulled him into the house. Then she picked up a packet on the coffee table and placed it in his hands.

"An airline ticket," he said, slightly confused.

"A one-way ticket to Toronto," she told him. "I was going to be on the plane this afternoon. You're right, Alan. It makes more sense for us to live there."

He leaned down to brush a warm kiss over her full lips. "I think we should discuss this before we make any rash decisions."

"Okay." Her eyes sparkled. "How about if we discuss it in front of the fireplace?"

"Rowena." He found it hard to draw breath. "When I thought I'd lost you…" He shook his head. "I wish I could find the words to tell you how I feel about you. Saying I love you just doesn't seem like enough."

"It's more than enough." She reached for his hand and placed it gently on her stomach. "But don't talk now. Just listen."

A tiny kick landed against his palm.

"Well?" she asked, a mischievous dimple flashing

in her cheek. "Can you decipher what our baby is trying to tell you?"

Our baby. He realized this was the first time she had said those words. She'd referred to it as *the* baby and *her* baby. Even *his* baby. But never *ours.* Until now. Alan shook his head, too overwhelmed to speak.

"Then I'll translate." Her voice grew husky. "We love you, Daddy."

A WEEK LATER, Rowena and Alan gathered their friends and family in the spacious gathering room of Twin Oaks. Fresh flowers graced every tabletop, and enticing aromas emanated from the dining room.

"We have an announcement to make," Alan said, circling his arm around Rowena's waist. His gaze scanned the crowd of guests. "Although I think a few of you may have already heard the news."

Several people nodded and exchanged knowing grins.

He slanted a smile toward his beautiful bride. "Two days ago, Rowena and I eloped to Pittsfield and got married."

Applause and happy laughter filled the air as Alan leaned down to kiss her. Rowena wrapped her arms around him and enthusiastically returned his kiss as the applause turned into raucous cheers. Then they both pulled away with embarrassed smiles.

"I love you so much," he murmured, to the sound of corks popping.

"I've never been happier," Rowena said, lifting on her toes to kiss him again. Right before she closed her eyes, she glimpsed his father beaming at them. Alan had introduced them earlier, when they'd arrived at Twin Oaks. She already liked George Rand, and it was easy to see how proud he was of his son.

Alan leaned close to her ear. "Can you believe how many people showed up here today?"

"Yes," she replied, knowing how people in a small town, especially Cooper's Corner, supported each other. She saw Ed Taylor talking chickens with Burt Tubb. Philo and Phyllis Cooper were asking state cop Scott Hunter and his wife, Laurel, about the string of burglaries in New Ashford. Alison Fairchild and Dr. Dorn's wife, Martha, stood admiring the antique spinning wheel in the corner of the room. And Keegan Cooper kept the twins occupied with magic tricks.

Beth Young, the town librarian, sat down at the piano and began to play a lilting sonata. Clint approached them with a tray full of champagne flutes. "Drinks for the bride and groom?"

Alan held up one hand. "We're having a baby, so champagne is off-limits."

Clint smiled. "I know. That's why we're serving sparkling grape juice today."

"You've thought of everything." Rowena took two flutes off the tray and handed one to Alan. "Thank you so much for allowing us to hold the reception here."

"It's our pleasure," Clint replied, setting the tray on a nearby table. "But you haven't told us yet if Cooper's Corner will need to start looking for a new barber."

Rowena glanced at her husband and saw him grin.

"We're not going anywhere," she told Clint. "Alan and I plan to raise our baby right here."

"That's right," Alan concurred. "Rowena's going to keep working at the shop, and I'm going to become a stay-at-home father."

"Really?" Maureen asked, walking up to them. "Lucky baby."

"Lucky me," Rowena said with a smile. "Alan sealed his own fate when he took over the house and the cooking while I was confined to bed. He's a natural at it."

"I love the publishing business," Alan explained, "but I lost my drive for a high-powered career three years ago. Now I want to concentrate on what's really important—like my new family. I'm looking forward to spending time with the baby and maybe even trying my hand at writing."

"A novel?" Maureen asked.

He shook his head, exchanging a meaningful glance with Rowena. "Actually, someone came up with a great idea for a nonfiction book. It will be written especially for expectant fathers. Everything a daddy-in-training needs to know."

"He's already talked to Dr. Milburn about providing the medical expertise for the book," Rowena added. "I think Alan will soon know more about pregnancy and babies than I do."

Clint reached out to shake his hand. "Good luck, and welcome to Cooper's Corner. I know you'll be a great addition to the community, Alan."

"Keegan's a great kid," Alan replied, "so it must be a good place to raise a family."

"It's time for the bride and groom to cut the wedding cake," Maureen announced. "Lori made it big enough to feed the entire village of Cooper's Corner."

As a line began to form at the cake table, Rowena glanced at her new husband and found him looking at her with unconditional love shining in his eyes. The baby moved inside her, and she marveled at the way fate had brought the two of them together.

A mistake at the Orr Fertility Clinic had turned out to be a miracle.

And the best part of all was that Rowena knew the miracles in their life together were just beginning.

EPILOGUE

CLINT AND MAUREEN cleared the last of the dishes off the buffet as the clock chimed midnight. Only a few slices of wedding cake remained, since so many of Cooper's Corner's residents had stopped in to congratulate the newlyweds and share in the celebration. A few stragglers remained, gathered around the fireplace as Dr. Dorn entertained them with stories about the early years of his medical practice.

"What a day," Maureen exclaimed, slumping against the kitchen counter. "I'm exhausted, but it was a beautiful reception. Don't Rowena and Alan make the perfect couple?"

"Looks like Cupid hit the mark with those two," Clint agreed, wiping his hands on a dish towel. "I'm just glad this weekend is finally over. All the guests have checked out, and the rooms are empty. So we're on our own for at least a little while."

"Let's enjoy it while we can," Maureen suggested, "and leave all these dishes until the morning."

"Good idea." He grabbed the coffeepot as they walked out of the kitchen. "I checked on the kids a few minutes ago. They're all sacked out in sleeping bags on the floor of your room. They made some kind of tent out of blankets."

Maureen smiled. "The girls were so excited when Keegan suggested an indoor camp out. I wonder if he realizes he's their hero."

"He's just a sucker for a pretty face." Clint grinned. "Just like his old man."

Maureen arched a speculative brow at her brother. "Any pretty face in particular appeal to you lately?"

He shrugged, then cocked his ear toward the gathering room. "Hey, I think Dr. Dorn is telling that great gallbladder story again."

"Very smooth," she teased. "Next time you want me to change the subject, just say so."

"All right," he said with a wink. "I will. Now I'd better go refill some cups."

She nodded as she moved toward the staircase. "I'll join you there in a few minutes. I want to check the guest rooms upstairs first and make sure all the lights are out."

The sound of familiar voices, now joined by Clint's deep laughter, drifted from the gathering room as she made her way up the stairs. It warmed her inside and out to know that they'd found a home here. Friends they could count on. Alan Rand was right—Cooper's Corner was the perfect place to raise a child.

Maureen switched on the hallway light when she reached the top of the stairs. The silence seemed almost eerie after the rush of guests they'd had this last month. She slowed her step as she walked by the door of the south bedroom. It was slightly ajar, which was strange. She usually kept the rooms locked when they were empty. Pushing the door open, she was surprised to see the bed she'd just made up this morning torn apart, the sheets and quilt in a tangled heap on top of the mattress.

Then she took a step closer and realized there was someone *in* the bed.

"Excuse me," she said, then cleared her throat. The body didn't move.

She stepped closer until she was able to see the pale face of a young woman half buried under one of the goose-down pillows.

"Hey," Maureen called more loudly, her cop's instincts kicking in. Something was very wrong here. She reached out to shake the woman's shoulder. "Wake up."

The woman didn't even twitch. Maureen shook her harder, practically yelling. "Are you all right?"

The woman's head lolled to one side, her body quivering unnaturally for a few moments. Then she stilled again, not once opening her eyes.

Maureen leaned down to pry one eyelid open, the stubby lashes thick with black mascara. The pupil was rolled back, which told her the woman must be unconscious.

Then she glanced over at the nightstand and saw the empty prescription bottle. She picked it up and read the label. Tamazepam. Sleeping pills.

She hurried from the room and called out for Dr. Dorn to join her upstairs. By the time he got there, the young woman had regained consciousness enough to empty her stomach into the wastebasket that Maureen held for her.

Dr. Felix Dorn was eighty-four years old, his narrow shoulders slightly stooped on his tall frame. As he sat down on the bed beside the woman, his perceptive blue eyes gleamed with concern.

"How are you feeling?"

The woman swallowed as she leaned weakly against the pillows. "A little better."

Dr. Dorn nodded, then picked up her slender wrist in his hand. "Your pulse is a little fast, but strong."

"Should I call the ambulance?" Maureen asked, tempted to call state trooper Scott Hunter as well.

"I don't think that will be necessary," Dr. Dorn replied as he checked the rest of her vital signs.

Maureen sensed her brother's presence behind her.

"Who is she?" Clint asked in a low voice.

Maureen shook her head. "I've never seen her before. I don't know who she is or how she ended up in one of our rooms."

The house had been filled with people all evening, some even going upstairs to tour the guest rooms. But no one had mentioned seeing an unconscious woman in one of the beds.

"Where am I?" the woman asked hoarsely, looking around the room with wary brown eyes.

"You're at the Twin Oaks Bed and Breakfast in Cooper's Corner, Massachusetts," Clint told her. "Do you remember how you got here?"

She shook her head. "I don't remember much. And I'm not sure if I dreamed it or if it was real."

Maureen took a step toward the bed. "What's your name?"

The young woman hesitated, as if she couldn't quite remember. "It's Trudi. Trudi Karr."

Dr. Dorn checked her pulse again, then patted her arm. "How old are you, Trudi?"

"Eighteen." Her voice was thready and her dark eyes huge in her face. She looked terrified. And so very young.

Something about her reminded Maureen of her daughters. "Where are you from?" she asked, wondering if the girl had a mother somewhere who was worried about her.

"New York." Trudi's gaze moved from her to Dr. Dorn. "What happened to me?"

"Don't you remember?" the doctor asked kindly.

She shook her head. "Everything feels…fuzzy."

Dr. Dorn held up the empty prescription bottle. "You took too many of these sleeping pills. If Maureen hadn't found you up here, you might not have made it."

Trudi struggled to sit up in the bed, but didn't have the strength. She slumped against the pillows. "No, I'd never do anything like that. I don't want to die."

"Then what happened?" Clint asked.

"I don't know," the young woman mused, rubbing the base of her throat with her fingers. "I left my home in Brooklyn because I was tired of my stepfather hitting me. I wanted to go to Buffalo, where my aunt lives."

"How did you plan to get there?" Maureen asked, knowing it was quite a distance. "A train? A bus?"

Trudi pushed back her short, limp brown hair. "No, I didn't have any money, so I decided to hitchhike. A guy picked me up in his truck. He seemed really nice."

Maureen suppressed a shiver at the teen's naiveté. She'd seen too many cases of runaways while on the police force in New York City. Runaways who fell victim to unscrupulous criminals who loved to prey on the young.

"Did this man hurt you in any way, Trudi?" Dr. Dorn asked, obviously sharing Maureen's concern.

"No," Trudi replied. "I was hungry, and he promised to buy me some food the next time he stopped for gas. We drank coffee out of his thermos and talked for a while." She looked at them, a frown wrinkling her brow. "My mind is so fuzzy. What could have happened?"

Clint's gaze flicked to his sister. "We're not sure."

"Do you know this man's name?" Maureen asked her. "Maybe we can track him down and find out the rest of the story."

"I only know his first name," Trudi replied. "He told me to call him Owen."

Maureen's heart thundered in her chest. "Owen?"

She saw Clint's jaw tense. "Can you describe him?"

Trudi thought about it for a moment. "He's about your height," she said, nodding toward the elderly doctor, "but younger. With dark hair that's thinning on top and dark eyes. That's all I really remember."

It was enough. Maureen's knees gave out, and she sagged onto the end of the bed. Owen Nevil had found her.

Clint walked over to her, giving her shoulder a reassuring squeeze. He knew about Owen's vow to hunt her down. Knew the man was obsessed with wreaking revenge on the woman who had sent his brother to jail.

"I still don't understand why I'm here," Trudi said, unaware of the bomb she'd just dropped.

But Maureen knew why. Owen Nevil had finally found her, and he wanted her to know it. He'd left Trudi here as his calling card, almost killing the poor girl.

Just like he wanted to kill her.

*Welcome to Twin Oaks—the new B and B
in Cooper's Corner. Some come for
pleasure, others for passion—and
one to set things straight...*

COOPER'S CORNER
*a new Harlequin continuity series
continues in February 2003 with
FOR THE LOVE OF MIKE!
by Muriel Jensen*

The cozy Twin Oaks B and B...a perfect retreat for divorced dad and dentist Michael Flynn to kick back over spring break with his two young daughters—and his Saint Bernard. Single mom and supermarket cashier Colleen O'Connor had the same idea for her and her two little boys...and their Siamese cat. Bad combination! No sooner had they arrived than the rain began, the kids started bawling, and the cat went after the dog. Even Mike and Colleen were fighting—their attraction!

Here's a preview!

CHAPTER ONE

HE PASSED THROUGH the common room and turned the corner to the sunporch, a little surprised to find it in darkness. He reached for the light switch, but a soft, small hand came down on his with surprising power, stopping the action. He caught the scent of flowers.

Hands took a firm hold of his arm and pushed him deeper into the room and away from the door. He didn't resist. This was too promising.

"Why, Mrs. O'Conner, you…" he began as he found himself in the dark corner between the wicker sofa and a bookshelf. But that same small hand covered his mouth.

"Don't speak!" Colleen whispered. "You've accused me of being a matronly coward, and it's my turn to rebut."

"I didn't…" he began, intending to remind her that he hadn't accused her of such behavior, just suggested she might think that of herself. But he was rendered silent again by soft flesh covering his mouth.

It wasn't her hand this time, though, but her lips.

While the fragrant darkness pulsed around him and laughter and quiet conversation came from the guest room, Colleen caught his face in her hands and kissed him with passion and ardor.

Surprise held him paralyzed, and she used it to her advantage. Her lips explored his, nudged and nipped at them until they parted, then she dipped the tip of an exploring tongue inside.

Meanwhile, her fingers went into his hair, causing a ripple of sensation along his scalp, down his spine. Her hands followed the line of his neck, across his shoulders and might have explored his back except that she didn't seem able to reach. They went down his arms instead, then up again, her right index fingertip exploring the rim of his ear, then tracing inside. It began to ring, as though his heart was calling for help.

Every nerve ending in his body was alive and quivering.

Her kiss drew out feeling from deep inside him, and the calm with which he'd handled his sexless life all this time was suddenly smashed to smithereens.

She nipped at his bottom lip one more time, then she dropped her hands to his shoulders, as though holding him in place.

"You super male types think that if a woman doesn't react to you," she said, keeping her voice down, obviously in deference to the guests just beyond in the guest room, "it's because she lacks desire. It seems to escape you that she could be as hot as you are, but simply discerning and not attracted to you. So there. Remember that kiss and try to tell yourself I'm a coward, unable to attract and hold a lover."

She dropped her hands from him, the blissful moment suddenly and abruptly over. Or so she thought.

He saw her pale eyes in the shadows as she gave him one last, judicious look, then turned away.

He reached out blindly in the dark, caught a fistful of the back of her sweater and pulled her to him.

"If you're so discerning," he said softly, wrapping his arms around her as she tried to wriggle away, "I obviously mean something to you, or that kiss wouldn't have had such impact."

She looked momentarily at a loss, then tossed her head haughtily. "I'm just more skilled than you give me credit for."

"You are skilled," he granted her, "but your heartbeat's slamming against my chest. Don't tell me that meant nothing to you except proof of your prowess."

"It meant there's chemistry," she admitted after a moment. "It's built-in in most of us. It means nothing."

"If that was simply chemistry," he argued, "it was nuclear chemistry. Why are you trembling, if it means nothing?" He was going to make her admit she felt something for him if he had to keep her here all night.

FREE Bathroom Accessories

With proofs of purchase
from Cooper's Corner titles.

YES! Please send me my FREE bathroom accessory without cost or obligation, except for shipping and handling.

<u>In U.S., mail to:</u> **COOPER'S CORNER** P.O. Box 9047 Buffalo, NY 14269-9047	<u>In CANADA, mail to:</u> **COOPER'S CORNER** P.O. Box 613 Fort Erie, ON L2A 5X3

Name (PLEASE PRINT)

Address   Apt. #

City   State/Prov.   Zip/Postal Code

Enclosed are three (3) proofs of purchase from three (3) different Cooper's Corner titles and $1.50 shipping and handling, for the first item, $0.50 for each additional item selected.

Please specify which item(s) you would like to receive:

- ☐   Liquid Soap Dispenser
- ☐   Soap Dish
- ☐   Toothbrush Holder
- ☐   Drinking Cup

COOPER'S

CORNER

ONE PROOF
OF PURCHASE
CCPOP

093 KJJ DNC4   © 2002 Harlequin Enterprises Limited   CCPOP

They're strong, they're sexy, they're not afraid to use the assets Mother Nature gave them....

Venus Messina is...

#916 WICKED & WILLING
by Leslie Kelly
February 2003

Sydney Colburn is...

#920 BRAZEN & BURNING
by Julie Elizabeth Leto
March 2003

Nicole Bennett is...

#924 RED-HOT & RECKLESS
by Tori Carrington
April 2003

The Bad Girls Club...where membership has its privileges!

Available wherever

is sold....

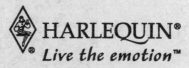

Visit us at www.eHarlequin.com

There's something for everyone...

Behind the
Red Doors

From favorite authors

Vicki Lewis Thompson

Stephanie Bond

Leslie Kelly

A fun and sexy collection about the romantic encounters
that take place at The Red Doors lingerie shop.

**Behind the Red Doors—
you'll never guess which one leads to love...**

Look for it in January 2003.

Corruption, power and commitment...

TAKING THE HEAT

A gritty story in which single mom and prison guard Gabrielle Hadley becomes involved with prison inmate Randall Tucker. When Randall escapes, she follows him— and soon the guard becomes the prisoner's captive... and more.

"Talented, versatile Brenda Novak dishes up a new treat with every page!"

—*USA TODAY* bestselling author Merline Lovelace

brenda novak

Available wherever books are sold in February 2003.

HARLEQUIN®
Makes any time special ®

Welcome to Twin Oaks—
the new B and B in Cooper's Corner.
Some come for pleasure, others for passion—
and one to set things straight...